MW01164885

# WESTERNS:
# WARPATHS &
# PEACEMAKERS

## ED GARRON

### Six Complete Novellas

### WILDCARD WESTERNS

ISBN 9781521047637

Dernford Press© Ed Garron/G Denny November 2018
The moral right of Ed Garron as author of this book has been asserted.

Published by Wildcard Books, & The Dernford Press, UK,
PO Box 123 London, England
& Seattle USA
Edition 1 Imprint 1.

Set in 'constantia' & U.S. standard English by J M Services


COVER ILLUSTRATION:
Copy of C M Russell original by Cody Barnard, with the permission of the artist (PD)

## PUBLISHERS NOTE:

### About the author:-

Ed Garron is an old-fashioned story teller pure and simple. He sticks to the conventions of western fiction pioneered by the likes of Louis L'Amour, Zane Grey, and J T Edson. Thus, his stories might depict the lone figure confronted by evil, or huge odds, or intrepid pioneers surviving through comradeship, skill, courage, and familiarity with firearms.

But there are elements that put Garron apart: set in the wilderness of the old western frontier, his plots, though thoroughly entertaining, have the unmistakable ring of truth about them.

"I like to use details of events that really happened," explains Garron, "especially the unusual ones that seem to defy logic, such as the cross-gun draw in Book One. As to the use of tricks in duals, there were many instances and variations. Other bizarre events, such as a white man bringing up a family in an Indian camp, as in Book Two, are perhaps better known; but, regarding the harsh penalty for stealing an Indian trapper's goods shown in Book Three, I have come across only one terrifying example, and repeat it here in all its gruesome details." (Read 'WARPATHS & PEACEMAKERS' to see what it entailed!)

Well, here they are: six complete novellas each with their own peculiarly fascinating characters, and those trademark twists and turns that will keep you turning the pages to the very end... enjoy!

**James Marsden, Editor WILDCARD WESTERNS, SEATTLE.**

# ALSO BY **ED GARRON:**

## WESTERNS 2: WILD AS THE WIND!
Six novellas of the Old West & Civil War...

## WESTERNS 3: BROTHER OF THE WOLF!
'Between Kurt Danvers and death stood a fire of pine,
two pieces of canvas and the will to live.'

## WESTERNS 4: YARNS OF THE OPEN RANGE
True and tall tales of life in the old cattle country.

www.edgarron.com

# CONTENTS:

## BOOK ONE...
# CROSS-GUN CAIRNS

## BOOK TWO...
# BIGFOOT BRIGGS

## BOOK THREE...
# WARPATHS & PEACEMAKERS

## BOOK FOUR...
## THE PRAIRIE THIEF

## BOOK FIVE...
## HANGIN' FEVER

## BOOK SIX...
## THE MAN FROM FORT DEFIANCE

# BOOK ONE...

# CROSS-GUN CAIRNS

*'Shooting at a man who is returning the compliment means going into action with the greatest speed of which a man's muscles are capable, but mentally unflustered by an urge to hurry or the need for complicated nervous and muscular actions which trick shooting involves.'*

Wyatt Earp

# CROSS-GUN CAIRNS

## CHAPTER I:
## A SIMPLE TRICK OF THE TRADE

**Sheriff Jem Fitzpatrick shouldn't have gone after Cross-Gun Cairns alone. But, the way he saw it, the man at the cards table was already wanted for two murders and had to be stopped – there and then.**

Cairns had taken the life of a farmer who wouldn't hand over a horse not a mile out of town. Before that he'd held up a mail-coach and killed a guard. Now he was sitting, bold as brass, playing poker in the Gold Bar Saloon, drinking whiskey and studying his hand as if nothing at all had happened. He was a reckless, ruthless, evil son of a bitch who feared no man. It might just as well have been the devil himself sitting in there, for all the heed he gave to the reputation of the fearless Fitzpatrick brothers.

So, as Jem buckled on his custom Remington .44 short-barreled pistols with the intention of taking Cairns to jail, for once he felt a little nervous – though his face gave away no inkling of it – and considered delaying his short walk down Main Street to the town's only drinking establishment until his brother got back in town.

But then he thought better of it. He knew that with or without his hot-shot young deputy, the people of Sanders Creek expected their man to make an arrest – without delay. That was what they paid him for. Townsfolk everywhere were

7

watching and waiting to see what he would do. And so, in the manner of speaking, were a whole host of unsavory characters in and around the town. Sure, the county had been quiet of late, but that didn't mean the old troublemakers had mended their ways. They were compliant; but the leopards hadn't changed their spots. Instead, they waited. Any sign of weakness was sure to embolden those who resented the proper enforcement of the law. It wouldn't take much for the bad old days to return to Sanders Creek – a desperado or two pushing their luck, a sheriff who wasn't quite up to his job.

It had happened elsewhere. But in this small town, people trusted Jem Fitzpatrick, had seen him stand his ground on more than one occasion when lesser men might have backed off or ridden out of town.

That Jem Fitzpatrick was not lacking in courage was never in doubt. Fast gunplay, however, was not the sheriff's strong point. Like most sheriffs, he was more a scattergun than a pistols man, you might say. In any kind of a fire-fight he needed his kid brother Stevie to even things up. The nineteen-year-old deputy could draw a gun like a gnarled old gunfighter. He could put a hole in a tossed up tin can before it hit the ground using his left or right Remington .36 Navy. With accuracy like his, he had no need for the heavier calibers. And he brandished his irons with a grim, eyes-narrowed determination that belied his years and made you think he would actually pull the triggers when needed. You couldn't say that about every deputy in the wild country. Some of them were a little less than reliable when the going got hot.

Yet, though Stevie Fitzpatrick could hit a moving target, give the evil-eye to bar-room drunks, and had escorted a few bad men to jail, his speed on the draw in a real one-on-one remained untested. That kind of caper was reserved for all-in tussles with out and out gunslingers. Men with little regard for their own lives, and even less for the lives of others.

Men like George Herbert Cairns.


*"Come quietly, Cairns,"* was Jem's fair warning. The sheriff already had a pistol trained on the outlaw, but even that didn't necessarily give him the edge he needed.

"All right, you got me," said Cairns slyly, rising from the card table and holding up his hands for all to see. "I'll come quietly, only I'll need a lawyer."

"Oh we'll find you a lawyer," said Jem Fitzpatrick, relaxing a little at the thought of Cairns in a courtroom. "Now toss those guns on the floor, real easy now."

Cairns removed the left gun and dropped it. He reached for the other, the right side one, with his right hand, then paused for a second. He began to cough and splutter in big convulsions, and bent over somewhat as if to control his fits of wheezing. Apologetically, it seemed, he held up his right hand with the palm open. But at that first cough, before he'd raised his hand, he'd pushed back the hammer of his remaining Colt – still in its holster – with a deft, practised movement of his thumb, thus leaving it cocked and ready to be touched off, when drawn, by the tiniest of pulls on its hair-trigger. Furthermore, the holster was on the *front* of Cairns' right thigh, not to the side, with the butt angled to the *left*!

Jem Fitzpatrick cottoned on immediately that he was being drawn into a trick, but reacted a second too slowly – and a second is a long, long time in a gunfight. Quick as the strike of a rattlesnake, Cairns left hand seized his remaining pistol in a wicked cross-gun draw and fired. The butt was no more than an inch above its (greased) holster as the bullet sped on its lethal errand, and his right hand, the one that had taken the sheriff's attention for a split second, was still held out open-palmed in apology.

The sheriff fell, lung-shot and dying, unable to use his gun, which fell on the floor beside his face. He had to watch what happened next.

Cairns, smiling and sniggering to himself, picked up his winnings, retrieved his own dropped gun, and backed out toward the saloon doors, covering the company of drinkers and fellow gamblers with his twin ivory-handled Colts as he left. He paused to scoop up the sheriff's short-barreled Remington .44 from the floor – a fine keepsake. At the doors he stopped, passing his gun-sights over anyone in the saloon crowd who so much as twitched a muscle, before edging out into the street. Even as he walked down the muddy sidewalk, he remained vigilant, wary of any citizen seeking to avenge the lawman.

But he needn't have worried. None fancied the challenge. Cairns, therefore, was left to escape scot-free, taking his horse from the livery after saddling it at leisure, and making off across the prairie and into the badlands, seeking a place where his kind was welcome.

Larsonville fitted the bill – a den of thieves and robbers if ever there was one. It had crooked gambling, illegal liquor, prostitution, gunplay, murder, you name it, and a bent town marshal who offered sanctuary to absolutely anybody and his dog for just a few pieces of silver.

As for the younger Fitzpatrick, by the time he got back in town, his brother's body was already in the undertaker's tender care. The best he could do was see that his brother got a decent funeral and a fine headstone. Losing Jem like that finally brought home the reality of being a lawman in the west: low pay for big risks, zero support from townsfolk when things turned ugly.

Blaming himself for his brother's death (having been out of town chasing a farm-girl who subsequently ditched him) Stevie Fitzpatrick resigned his job and headed north-west trailing his brother's killer. But two weeks out, Cairns seemed to vanish into thin air on the edge of the Utah badlands.

By this time exhaustion, hunger and poverty had taken their toll on the former deputy. There was nothing to be done for the time being except survive, which meant working for a living. With one ear open for word of Cross-Gun Cairns, last seen Hooper's Flats, Utah, Stevie Fitzpatrick changed his name to Henderson and became a cowpuncher, and a good one at that. The Bar Z men nick-named him 'Stoop' on account of his stance when drawing a gun. Leaning well forward and bending from the waist, the stooping man drew so fast to smash the bottles they placed on fence-posts that tongues began wagging that 'Stoop' was maybe a little too handy with those well-oiled Remington .36's – the ones he wore a little too low on the thighs when he rode into town.

Whenever a posse was got up in nearby One Dog Creek, he took time off his job on the Bar Z ranch to play his part. Evidently, the thrill of confronting outlaws had not left him; and the hope of catching up with Cairns was always foremost in his thoughts. Once, he accompanied a sheriff from Colorado he met in town, a man on a mission called Davis McNamara, all the way up to Montana. There, the pair of them gunned down three men wanted for the killing of a deputy and some bank-clerks in Durango. They were desperate men with prices on their heads – though Cairns was not among them.

But Stevie's luck was about to change. That mean snake Cairns was about to cross his path. When Cairns had seemingly 'disappeared', he had only gone a town or two further on, a mere thirty miles west from where Fitzpatrick lost his trail. Given that the Bar Z Ranch was flush with money and fat cattle, Cairns was bound to turn up there someday, like a moth to a candle. Even in a big territory like Utah, men like Cairns, and men like Stevie Fitzpatrick were almost certain to meet sooner or later. The one evil and negative, a force for ill, destined to prey off honest money, the other, a young man with a chip on his shoulder and an instinct for putting the wrongs of the world aright. Polar opposites of the law, you might say.

Small wonder, then, that one day the pair would find themselves in the same place, at the same time, both spoiling for a fight – and neither likely to back down.

# CHAPTER TWO:
# THE HOLD-UP

There was only one touch of green in the whole vast panorama of prairies, a small patch of cottonwoods and pines upon the banks of a small stream which ran through the plain to merge with the sluggish waters of the river in the badlands towards the west. It was late summer, hot, dusty, the time of pesky flies and no rain. Consequently, the stream was low, slow, and muddy.

In the shade of a tall pine, with his back against a tree trunk, sat a red-bearded man with small, piggy eyes. He bore the patient, tolerant look of one who waits. Short, burly and bull-necked, there were suggestions of strength about the man. A few paces away a horse was tethered. The animal was saddled and the cinch had been loosened, but now the man went to the horse and tightened it. He turned and stared steadily toward the north, where a swirl of dust arose from the hot, dry surface of the trail.

The man untied the horse and led it to a spot close to where the track crossed the little stream. Here he re-tied his mount, turned, and dropped his hands to the ivory butts of his guns. He gazed northwards. The cloud of dust grew nearer, and he was soon able to make out the shape of two horses, but not, as yet, any riders. Then, a square brown object behind the trotting animals came into view.

It was a buckboard. Soon, two figures could be seen perched on its seat.

"Thought so," muttered the man beside the road. "Too

valuable a cargo to put on a horse on this trip. Well, that thing jus' makes it easier for me."

The buckboard came on at a good speed and presently reached a straight piece of road leading directly to the ford over the creek.

As it approached it slackened speed. The man at the reins had doubtless seen the mud where the road crossed the stream. He continued to slow his horses, then suddenly two reports of a Spencer 56-56 carbine sent bullets whining off rocks in the road and he pulled up – real sharp.

The gunman roared:

"Put 'em up, and you on the left, lay off that shotgun mister! One more inch and I'll plug yer! Don't make me do it."

The guard withdrew his hand from near the shotgun propped up beside him. The other man, the driver, looked sideways at his guard. One glance at the quaking fellow told him all he needed to know, that the robber was not going to be challenged today.

"Up high boys, right up where I can see 'em," shouted the gunman.

The driver and guard did as the outlaw commanded.

"Now get down off there on my side, one at a time and don't forget where yer hands belong."

The man with the guns lined his two prisoners up beside the cart and kept them covered with his rifle.

"You've got somethin' in there that I want," he snapped. "Git it out. Be quick!"

"The mail?" faltered the driver, "The mail? I'll hand it

14

yer..."

His face had turned a chalky white.

"You know I don't want the mail," was the savage rejoinder.

The driver looked helplessly at his guard, whose hands were now shaking uncontrollably. "Give him the mail, Clyde..."

A shot rang out and a chunk of wood from the side of the buckboard next the driver flew into the air along with some splinters. By the time the two men had flinched and re-opened their eyes the outlaw had worked the lever and the Spencer was ready to fire again.

"Quit that chatter," said the red-bearded man. "I know yer carryin' the money for the Bar Z cattle sold last week, an' I don't aim on asking you fellers agin."

The driver climbed hastily into the back of the cart and picked up a plain-looking wooden chest with a lock on it.

"It's too heavy for yer horse," whined the driver apologetically.

"Sling it down," ordered the rifleman, "and get back next to yer pal. Pronto, I'm losing patience."

A single shot broke off the lock.

The robber soon had the several thousand dollars in his saddlebags.

"Not too heavy now," he growled.

He threw the guard and driver's weapons into the creek.

"All right, now git in, an' git goin'. Don't even *think* of gittin' them guns out o' the crick. Go back the way yer come, real steady, or I'll knock the pair of yer off that seat for fun.

Gallop them horses in my sight, an' I'll plug yer."

He fired a warning shot in the air to show that he meant business.

The buckboard went ambling back down the dusty road at a snail's pace, with the two men hunched in the seat not daring even to glance back over their shoulders; but if they had, they would have seen no trace of the bearded man, for he was already long gone, struck out across country for Larsonville, one of those godforsaken little mining towns you might come across just before the higher peaks barred your way west.

"Waal, he sure made fools of us," whined the driver. "Got all that cash and th'ain't much chance of gittin' it back. But did y'see that fancy rig with a gun on the front o' his leg? That was Cross Gun Cairns, that was. We're lucky to be alive."

"Yep," said his companion, "We've bin skinned by the most wanted man in the territory. If he'd drawn one of them pistols, reck'n we'd both be chewin' on dirt right now. Folks say every time he draws iron, some poor sucker gets it. Ain't no sheriff round these parts goin' after him neither, 'less he got twenty men o' more."

"Sheriffs? Don't make me laugh," said the driver, sourly. "We won't be seeing no lawman hot-footin' it after him any time soon, mark my words."

"Nope. That's for sure," said the guard. "Specially not Hal Peters. He's got more excuses than a Mormon virgin in a hayloft – and that's a fact!"

# CHAPTER THREE:
## THE RIGHT MAN FOR THE JOB

Hal Peters, the elderly sheriff of One Dog Creek, angrily paced his office, chewing the end of an unlit cigar. He was gray-haired, gray-bearded and slightly lame in his gait on account of a bullet that had passed through his back a long time ago. Now and then he paused to look at the other man in the room, who sat beside the sheriff's desk rocking his chair back and forth on two legs.

"So now we got Cross-Gun Cairns on our doorstep an' he's making a damn fool of me, Morton," the sheriff thundered. "Couldn't you find any trace of him at all?"

Deputy Sheriff Bud Morton, a spare, angular-faced fellow of late middle-age, shook his bald-pated head sleepily.

"Followed him up the side of a hill headin' east into the badlands, Hal, then lost his trail two miles on. Might've vanished into thin air, horse an' all, far as I'm concerned. Bet he's gone to Larsonville. A man in the saloon says he's got friends over there, includin' the marshal."

"Dutchy Smith's no marshal!" said Peters. "He's just some half-drunken gunslinger the miners roped into the job for a few bags of their silver. He'd jus' as soon shoot you as look at you."

"Well, the word is that Cairns is in cahoots with him, an' has a few more pals besides," yawned Morton, picking up a match off the table.

"Waal, that figures, I bet he's made lots an' lots of friends there, Bud," said Peters frowning, "an' one of these days I'll

17

pay 'em a visit an' clean up the whole damn nest o' rattlesnakes. Only–"

Morton raised one eyebrow, knowing what came next.

"Only with this here back of mine I can't ride out for a while, an' till then I'm stuck in Dog Creek. Can't ride out with a back like mine. Not for a while, anyhow."

"Uh-huh," said Morton, rocking himself gently while carefully examining the matchstick.

"Yep," said Peters, "One of these days I'll flush 'em out, see if I don't! They'll be real sorry they chose them badlands to air their bunch o' dirty tricks."

"They say Cairns's real fast, though, Hal," said the deputy, the matchstick now waggling in his mouth as he spoke, "Quick as lightnin' with both hands, and he's got a trick."

"Oh sure, he's got a trick all right," said Peters looking out the window. "Folks say he straightens up and makes as if to go, and then turns to shoot with a mean cross-gun draw – like this!"

Peters whipped round and pulled his colt .44 on Morton with his left hand.

"Uh-huh," said the deputy, "Like that – only maybe an itsy-bit faster."

Morton grinned slowly, and winked at his boss.

The sheriff reddened at his assistant's little joke.

"Waal, ain't nobody bested ol' Hal Peters yet," said the Sheriff, putting away his pistol, even more riled than before. "An' I don't see him a-comin' into *my* town."

"True," said Morton, "an' that's mebbe lucky for us, 'cos

18

he's one mean son of a bitch. They say he killed a dozen men at least. We've good reason to be a little wary of a man like that."

"He won't be easy to take, for sure. Got a poster with his ugly mug on it today. He's up to three thousand now. He's got the worst record in the territory, and that's a fact; but how'm I gonna' get him? I can't cover the whole of this here county by myself. An' I can't send you with a posse till I know for certain where he is."

"Send *me* with a posse?" said Morton, the matchstick falling out of his mouth. "Why hell, I'm more'n willin' to go with a posse, jus' say the word, if that's what you want, Hal, only-"

"Wait – now I'm thinkin' it's mebbe more of a job for one man," said Peters scratching his chin.

"A single man, Hal?" said Morton, his forehead furrowed with concern. "In Larsonville? You sure? Well, hell yes, I'll beat it out to Larsonville an' hang on till I get Cairns – only he'll likely be warned as soon's I hit town an' then..."

His voice trailed off.

"Yep – you're right. He'll get you, easy as pie," said the sheriff. "Guess he knows your face already."

"He knows *both* of us, come to that," said Morton, "after we stood right next to the varmint at a cattle-sale and still didn't cotton on."

He casually tossed a mangled matchstick into the bin.

"Yep," said the sheriff, "We were slow off the mark that day an' now he seen us. What's needed is a new face. But who's handy enough to take that coyote down? Who do we know who's got the sand?"

The two men suddenly looked at each other:

*"Henderson!"* they said simultaneously.

The sheriff added, almost apologetically:

"Folks will likely say we used him – him bein' only a cowpuncher, but hell – he's flash with a pistol, and a face the Larsonville crowd – including our friend Cairns – don't know yet. He's a cool customer too."

"Yep," said Morton, helping himself to another matchstick from the case on the desk, "he's a cool one all right. Heck, they say he knocked them two rustlers over last month 'fore either one'd cleared leather."

"If I didn't know better," said the sheriff, "and if he wasn't such a nice young feller, I'd say he was an out and out gunslinger."

"Or a lawman," said Morton, biting down on his match.

"He will be," said the sheriff, "when I swear him in. Jus' hope we don't get the man killed doin' our business."

"If he volunteers," said Morton, "he's goin' of his own accord – and for the three thou reward, of course."

"Well, there's that to it," said the sheriff. "That kind o' money could set a man up for life round here – get him his own spread."

"Or a fancy plot over there on Tomb Hill," said Morton.

They were silent for half a minute, weighing it up. Presently, Peters turned to his man and said:

"Damn it, Bud, we *got* to send him; if anyone can do it, Stoop Henderson can. He's the real deal."

"I agree. Some say he's been close to the edge of what's

lawful himself," said Morton. "That'd put him in good stead on a job like this."

"Doubt he ever went agin' a badge," said the sheriff; "He's not the type. As for him breakin' the law, well, no-one ever complained to me. Even them rustlers he took down were reachin' for their pieces – if that's his sort of game, well hell, I'm all for it."

"Likewise," said Morton. "Shall I go find him, boss?"

"Tomorrow night," said Peters, examining his empty match-case, "he'll be drinkin' in the Golden Spur with the Bar Z crowd. Take him on one side an' tell him I want to see him here in my office. Early's best – 'fore folks start gettin' a little too lively, if you catch my drift. And Bud–"

"Yes, boss?"

"Take yourself down to the general store an' get me some more matches. I've a mind to smoke my cigar now."

# CHAPTER FOUR:
## THE ONE MAN POSSE

"How long have you known Cross-Gun Cairns was in Larsonville and not told me?" said Stoop Henderson angrily as he stood in Hal Peter's office all clean-shaven and spruced up for his Saturday night.

"An' why should we think you'd be so interested in him?" said Peters.

"N-No reason," said Stoop, recovering his cool, "But how long?

"Well, couple of months mebbe. Been mooching around the badlands a deal longer I'd say. No reason to crow about it, till yesterday when he came an' snatched your boss's cash. Take it he ain't told you yet."

"Nope. But that's his business. So you pick *me* out to get Cairns instead of goin' yourselves – or gettin' up a posse mebbe. I'd like to know why."

Peters and Morton eyed each other uneasily.

"Waal, to be forthright," said the sheriff, "you're mor'n handy with those Remingtons an' he an' his pals don't know your face."

"Uh-huh," said the cowpuncher as he rolled himself a smoke, "and what exactly do you figure I should do, when me an' Cairns an' all his pals comes face to face? You're the sheriff, so you must know. Now please, do tell."

The cowpuncher raised his eyebrows, looking first at the sheriff, then at the deputy, waiting for an answer.

"Waal, I g-guess I don't exactly know, I mean..." stuttered

Hal Peters.

"Uh-huh," said Stoop, "Seems to me you've set me up for some long-shot mission while you two sit idly by smoking fat cigars and chewin' matches."

He scraped his match across the sheriff's desk, adding yet another scratch to its battered surface, and lit his cigarette.

"If you put it like that," said the sheriff, shame-faced, "it don't sound so clever. Sorry I put you on the spot. I shouldn't have asked. It was wrong of me."

"Yep," said Henderson, "Damn straight it was. Can't think what got into you, askin' a cowpoke to do your dirty work like that. You two should be darned ashamed of yourselves."

Morton and Peters looked at each other uncomfortably.

"Look, no hard feelings Stoop," said the deputy, "let me buy you a drink. C'mon boss, it's Saturday night, we'll take a turn down to the Golden Spur with this man."

"I'm sorry," said the cowpuncher, "but I can't go drinking with you boys, I got things to do."

"Now don't be like that," said the sheriff, "We only thought–"

"Peters, you ain't hearing me straight. I've no objection to drinkin' with you, in fact I look forward to it. But first I'm ridin' over to Larsonville. I'm goin' now, and I'll be ridin' all night."

"But why Stoop, after all you said, why go an' put yourself on the line if you think the way you do?" said Morton.

Stoop drew deeply on his cigarette so that almost a half of it turned to glowing ash, then exhaled with a long sigh that filled half the room with smoke.

"Waal now boys, seems you two jus' got lucky," he said. "You ever heard of a sheriff called Jem Fitzpatrick?"

"Every lawman's heard of him," said Hal Peters. "He was a brave man, everyone said so. One of Cairns early victims, sorry to say. But what's that to you, Henderson?"

"The names not Henderson. I'm Stevie Fitzpatrick. So don't go puttin' the wrong name on them deputy's papers."

At this, the lawmen's jaws dropped open.

It was a while before Morton was able to speak:

"So you're Jem Fitzpatrick's kid brother! That sure explains a couple o' things."

"Oh yeah? Like what, for instance?" said Stoop.

"Waal now," said Morton, "The way you handle your irons, for one. That trip to Colorado. The attitude too, mebbe."

"It must have been gnawin' away in your guts," said Peters, shaking his head at the irony of it all, "Waitin' for a chance to get Cairns, and we go ask you to find him in Larsonville. What are the odds o' that?"

"Never mind the odds," said Stoop, "Jus' get me them papers."

"Wait," said the sheriff, "Hold your horses, man. Mebbe we can't send you, now, can't you see? You'd never be able to keep your cool, not on this job. I mean, the man murdered your brother. Nope, I'm gettin' up a posse first thing Monday, that's final."

24

"A posse is it now, huh?" laughed Fitzpatrick, rolling his eyes in impatience; "First you say you want me to get Cairns, next you're pussyfootin' around as if you give a damn, and now it's got to be a posse! Exactly what kind of a sheriff are you, Peters? Seems to me we need to get a few things straight-"

"Now hold on a minute, young feller," said Peters, "No need to be like that-"

"No, goddammit!" snarled Fitzpatrick, banging his fist on the desk, "I *won't* hold on a minute, and I *will* be like that! Now put them papers on the table and read me that oath, Peters, 'cos I'm leavin' in five minutes flat!"

A few minutes later, as his new deputy ambled from the office, Peters followed him outside, calling out in a phoney-cheerful voice:

"Be seeing you, Stoop, reckon you're-"

"Spare me the compliments and the small-talk," snapped Fitzpatrick. "If what they say about Cairns is true, it's a one-way trip, an' you know it."

"If you feel that way, Stoop, then why do the job?" said Peters stupidly.

"You know why," hissed Stoop over his shoulder, as he slowly walked back down the street to get his horse.

Five minutes later, Fitzpatrick was already on the trail to the badlands, feeling more alone and vulnerable than he'd ever felt in his life.

# CHAPTER FIVE:
## HELL OF A RECKONING

On the long, moonlit ride across the badlands, Fitzpatrick rehearsed his plan of stealth and surprise.

"A shot in the back is plenty good enough for the likes of him," he thought. "I'll come at him from the back of the saloon while he's drinkin'. Or mebbe I'll plug him while he's sleepin', to make quite sure I get him. But if he's ready, an' sees me, I'll try a trick. Don't care if he gets me too, jus' so long's I knock him over for Jem."

He smiled grimly to himself at the thought of Cairns lying dead in the sawdust of a bar-room floor. All night long the thought kept him going, as he pressed his mount along at a fast trot.

At first light he spurred his horse into a gentle lope, and gave him only short rests every hour; even so, it was not until three in the afternoon that he reached his destination. It had been cruel on the horse, and the gelding would be weeks recovering from the trip, but it had to be done.

He gave his exhausted mount to a weasel of a man in the Larsonville livery, and was directed to The Silverado, where, he was told, Cairns was sure to be sitting on a Sunday, playing cards and swigging the stuff the barman made on his still at the back of the premises.

He looked in over the doors and saw his man in the middle of the room, surrounded by the biggest, ugliest bunch of cut-throats he'd ever seen in one place. There were enough weapons on view to re-arm the South and fight the Civil War again. Then there were the hidden ones to consider; and the barman would have to be watched too – he looked shifty and sly, and was bound to have a gun somewhere behind that counter.

He took a deep breath and tried to remember his best plan, but one look at the Cross-Gun Man and all his plans flew out the window.

Instead of walking round the back and stalking in from the kitchen, he found himself kicking open a door and stamping in.

"Hey Cairns," he said, putting on his badge, "Thought you might like somethin' shiny to aim at."

A man with a full red beard and piggy eyes looked round at him, annoyed, but in no way cowed.

"Oh yeah?" he said, "Sez who, exactly?"

"Guess."

"Waal now, ain't yer a funny one!" sneered the outlaw. "Maybe some heartbroken cowpoke with a cactus up his ass 'cos I killed his best pal – or a brother maybe."

"Uh-huh. You're mighty good at guessing, mister."

"Wait. That tin star! Only a deputy! Oh Lordy now, ain't I jus' quakin' in my boots. Now let's see. Would yer be Nathan Blake's young sidekick? Outer Santa Teresa mebbe?"

"Nope. Not even close," said Fitzpatrick.

"Ha! Now I got it. Thought I saw a resemblance – you'd be Jem Fitzpatrick's kid brother. The one that ran away."

"I ain't runnin' now."

"Waal, yer should be," said Cairns. "Yer sure talk tough, but yer needs to remember I've already plugged a dozen

27

young whippersnappers like you, Fitzpatrick."

"Uh-huh," said Stoop, adopting the body forward position to shoot that gave him his nick-name. "Like to try for thirteen, Cairns?"

"Sure. And even if yer gets me, my friends here will fill yer full of metal 'fore I hits the ground!"

"Doubt it," said Stoop, "I'll kill the first man that twitches. Maybe the second. Now stand up, quit yer yap, an' step away from that table."

"Yer a fool, Fitzpatrick, jus' like yer brother," said Cairns.

"An' you're a thievin' rattlesnake," said Stoop, "An' I shoots rattlesnakes."

"That so?" snarled Cairns, adjusting his holsters and clicking back the hammer of the right-side Colt with the back of his hand. He took his stance: upright, with the right hand hovering over that right gun, flexing his fingers, inviting Stoop to focus on it. But it was the left hand that Stoop was interested in. Why was it hanging innocently by a thumb on his belt, too high and wide for a quick cross-gun draw? It didn't make sense. Maybe the man was super-human. Or maybe his right would flash across and take the left-side gun. Wasn't this man named Cross-Gun Cairns?

The young man's eyes flicked between those hands, trying to work out where the trick was coming from; at the same time Stoop lurched sideways against a card table, causing the glasses on it to slide off and shatter on the floorboards.

Cairns' left hand whipped out his third gun from the holster under his coat and fired. Then he crumpled to the floor, a look of surprise and anger on his face. He was trying to speak, but no words came out.

"What's the matter, Cairns? Cat got your tongue?" said Fitzpatrick, a smoking short-barreled Remington .44 still in his left hand. Meanwhile, his two .36's were still sitting snug in their holsters.

Cairns' finger tried to point out, and his lips protest, that Stoop had somehow managed to mirror his own latest trick: a wicked, left-handed cross-gun draw from a *third* holster under a frock-coat. An identical trick, a simultaneous draw! But though the deputy's shot had been despatched at the same moment as Cairns', Fitzpatrick's aim had been marginally better. Stoop had a crease in his side, and was leaking a few drops of crimson onto the bar-room sawdust; Cairns, however, was lung-shot, hit squarely and slowly drowning in his own blood. Writhing on the floor, his face was a ghastly shade of white. He tried to speak, but the only thing leaving his mouth was bright red foam. And though a still-smoking gun had fallen in front of his face, his weakening hand couldn't reach it.

At that moment, a movement from the bartender caught Stoop's eye. Instinct took over and he felt the Remington buck in his hand.

The bullet smashed through a bottle of gut-rot liquor next to the bartender, showering him with splinters.

Sometimes practice pays off.

"Don't," said Stoop.

Cursing horribly, the bar-keep dropped his pistol on the bar. But the real danger came from the man who had just crept in the door.

"Freeze kid!" said Dutchy Smith, squinting over two cocked pistols at Fitzpatrick's back. "Now drop that gun. I'm the law round here, in case you didn't know, and I don't like two-bit bounty hunters sneakin' into my town."

Stoop froze, then lowered his gun-arm, but held on to the pistol. He knew that once disarmed, he was as good as dead. He began to turn.

"One more inch," shouted Smith, "and I fire. Now drop it!"

Stoop had no choice but to toss his gun on the floor. He turned. A toothless, jumpy-looking man with a bright scarlet face had him covered, no mistake. The man was hatless, showing a bald head from which rivulets of sweat were running down his face. The guns in his hands were shaking.

"Now the other," growled Smith, not twigging that the stranger had three pieces.

"No badge, marshal?" said Stoop, dropping his second gun.

"Don't need no badge," said Smith, taking a careful aim at the cowpuncher's heart, "I've been elected, you might say."

"Wonderful, thing, democracy," said Stoop, eying the motley bunch of cut-throats, thieves and vagabonds about him in the room.

Dutchy Smith's finger tightened on his trigger. Even as Fitzpatrick snatched the remaining gun from his left holster, he knew he would be too late.

The blast of a shotgun in the doorway sent Smith sprawling on the floor. His pistols went off as he fell, putting one hole in the floor near Stoop's foot, another in a table top on his other side.

There was the snap of a breech closing after a rapid reload, and in stomped Bud Morton with his still-smoking ten-gauge. He was chewing a match between his teeth, but for once, the sleepy look had left his face and he looked alert, mean, and mighty dangerous.

"Who's next?" said Morton, swinging his barrels from one ugly face to another, finally arresting them in the direction of the bar-keep.

There was no reply, no movement. He looked across at Stoop.

"Thought you might need a hand," he drawled. Then he caught sight of Cairns, now stock-still on the sawdust. "Looks like you already did the hard bit," he said.

Stoop picked up his own guns and took the ivory-gripped Colts from the dead man, then froze. The outlaw's third gun, the one on the floor, was a short-barreled Remington .44 identical to his own 'spare'. It took him a second or two to compute that both he and Cairns had been carrying one of Jem's pair as back-up, taken from him, for different reasons, on the day he died. Somehow both men had thought up the same trick, concealing guns from the same matching pair, and both used them on the same day! Full of confusion, he found himself mouthing the question:

"Sweet Jesus! What were the odds of that?"

A sick feeling came over Stevie Fitzpatrick. What would Jem think of him now? Killer? Gunslinger? A man who thought the same thoughts as George Herbert Cairns!

31

"My gunfightin' days are over, as of now," he thought to himself, "if it's only made me sink as low as that skunk."

Morton and Fitzpatrick backed out onto the street and untied two horses from the rail. Morton had taken the precaution of getting two fresh mounts from the livery and hitching them there in case a tactical retreat was necessary. They were skinny, dull-coated old nags, but they would get their riders safely home.

Taking his reins and preparing to mount, Fitzpatrick's face suddenly grew pale as death and his legs almost buckled beneath him. It was only with difficulty that he swung his leg over his mount and spurred the gelding into a lope. Morton saw the change in him, but said nothing until they were way out of town. They'd slowed to a steady trot and were riding over what passed for grass in that part of the world.

"You all right?" was all he asked.

It was a full ten minutes before Stoop made his reply.

"Didn't think it'd make me feel this way," he said simply.

"Uh-huh," said Morton, "And how exactly *do* you feel?"

"Sick to my stomach," said Stoop. "Empty. Ashamed."

Morton eyed his companion curiously.

"That man killed your brother," he said. "You'd a right to do what you did."

"You don't understand," said Fitzpatrick, "I enjoyed it – a bit too much. An' I hoodwinked him with the same low-down trick he tried to pull on me. I'm no better than *him*."

The deputy pursed his lips and gave a low whistle of surprise.

"We all got our reasons," said Morton, "An' our

methods. Takes somethin' powerful in a man to make him do what you did."

They rode on for a while in silence again.

"And you, Morton?" said Stoop at last, "Why'd you turn up an' risk your neck like that? You didn't need to come."

"It weren't right," said the deputy, "sending you off alone like that. The die were loaded agin' yer."

"Guess I got lucky," said Stoop, "This time. And thanks."

Morton placed a match between his teeth and squinted at the horizon. He'd been waiting for the right moment to say what was on his mind.

"One more thing," he said, turning to face Stoop, "Hal Peters resigned his post last night; turned in his badge to Bill Parks the Mayor."

"Good," said Stoop, "The man wasn't up to the job."

"Mebbe so," said Morton, "Old age an' law enforcin' don't exactly go hand in hand. Anyhow, when Parks hear'd I was goin' after you, he asked me to give you this. Says there's no-one else."

He showed Fitzpatrick the sheriff's badge in his hand.

"No-one else, huh?" said Stoop. "How very flatterin'."

"Your brother'd want you to take it," said Morton. "I'll help you out all I can, though, truth to tell, I'm gettin' a bit too long in the tooth for this game."

Stoop looked at Morton, then the badge, and blinked a couple of times, but said nothing. The two of them rode on another few strides, the heat-haze shimmering around them.

The shakiness had left Fitzpatrick now, and despite his wound, he felt different, good even. Something inside him had changed. It was the guilt, though he didn't know it, the guilt that had been eating away at his soul, all those years. It left him there and then. If the mayor, the town, and Bud Morton all trusted him to look after One Dog Creek, he felt duty-bound to do it. He wasn't a gunfighter; he saw that now. He wasn't a cowpoke either. He'd been a lawman all along. Slowly it dawned on him, how all that had happened to him in the past few years had led him to this one point in time, a rare moment when everything seemed to make sense.

Only the thought of killing held him back. What kind of a man enjoys the prospect of taking the life of a man? And did that make him as bad as a man like Cairns, or Dutchy Smith?

He weighed it all up in his mind. He even imagined asking his brother what he should do – it was not the first time he had settled a dilemma that way – and awaited the reply.

"Well?" said Morton, "What d'you say, Stoop? Still got some of that Fitzpatrick sand in yer gut?"

He laughed quietly to himself at the very thought of a Fitzpatrick lacking courage.

Stoop said nothing, only touched the short-barreled Remington .44 in his pocket – the one Cairns took from Jem – then turned to Morton, fixed him with steely eyes, stretched out his hand, and took the silver star.


THE END


34

# BOOK TWO...

# BIGFOOT BRIGGS

*'I was happy in the midst of dangers and inconveniences.'*
Daniel Boone

# BIGFOOT BRIGGS

## CHAPTER ONE:
## THE MAN IN THE GRIZZLY COAT

**They called him Bigfoot Briggs, and he mostly lived way up in the hills.**

Someone had given him the name after he arrived in the west, and it seemed to fit his size, his somewhat clumsy, lumbering gait, and the slowness of his movements.

By the look of him, huge in his bear-skin coat and wide-brimmed brown leather hat, you might be forgiven for thinking he had slightly less than average intellectual powers.

But you'd be wrong.

He'd been an officer in the army, graduating from West Point in 1859, but later returned to his family farm in Missouri, which he inherited on the death of his father. He later commanded a troop of cavalry in the Civil War, regular soldiers, not raiders. Which side he fought on is neither here nor there; but he saw an awful lot of killing, an awful lot of maiming, cruelty, and destruction.

Then, suddenly, he was free again. Instead of returning to the ruins of his farm, he headed west, and he didn't stop until he hit the mountains. There he became a trapper, a mountain man, a hunter who lived life on his own terms. He spoke five or six Indian dialects and was fluent in Indian sign language, which kept him alive in many a tricky encounter. There was no such thing as a solitary mountain man. Some men worked in heavily armed teams; others made peace and co-existed with the Indians. Briggs fitted into the latter category. It was the Wynoochee Indians of the far north-west who took him into their protection. They called him Wa-Ki-Chichna, meaning Man-Who-Is-Bear. At one of their higher camps, out of harm's way, he had a wife and children. The spoils he carried away from the stores, farms and wagons he encountered were mostly for them, to see them comfortably through the long, hard, frozen winters the higher parts of the Eastern Cascades produced each year.

That spring, in 1875, he emerged from the wilderness at O'Halloran's General Store, Hobson Pass, just outside of Leavenworth, up to no good, people thought, as usual. When he walked into the only shop of that tiny settlement that day, knocking a couple of metal skillets off a shelf as he went in, his grizzly coat, long beard and curious smell made people think a mythical creature from the hills was paying them a visit. Thus, his entry was greeted by a sudden silence. O'Halloran, peering at him through a haze of blue tobacco smoke, was the first to react, and summed up what everybody thinking when he said:

"Hallo! Who in heaven's name are you, big feller?"

The big man's jaw tightened, but he did not speak at first, but only spluttered and coughed in the cloud of smoke the shopkeeper and some of his customers was puffing out of their pipes. There were eight men and four women purchasing that day, their buckboards and carts lined up outside.

He looked the store over, noting all the things he needed

to pack on his mules, ignoring the pesky people present for the moment.

He took so long to answer, the others thought he wasn't going to speak. So they turned away from him to carry on with their own activities, a little uneasy that this great bear of a man was lumbering about the shop like a bigfoot come in from the cold.

"The name's Briggs," he said.

"What's that? Briggs you say?" said the store-keeper brightly, trying to be polite.

By this time some of the customers in the shop were snickering to themselves.

"Briggs, Bill Briggs," he said, "though folks do call me Bigfoot an' I don't mind it. Hev yer hear'd o' me?"

"Nope," said the shopkeeper. "Only bin here two months."

"I hev," said a little short man, with a little short wife, "I hear'd plenty about yer!"

"Yeah?" said Bigfoot Briggs, "All good, I'm hopin'."

"Some of it, I guess," mumbled the little man.

"Spit it out then," said Briggs. "What've yer hear'd?"

The little man cleared his throat nervously.

"I hear'd," he said anxiously, "that yer mainly surface t'other side o' the mountains, an' yer the best damn trapper in the country."

"That the good part?" said the giant. "Now let's hear the bad."

"Folks did say-"

But here the little man faltered.

39

The tiny woman suddenly chipped in:

"Folks did say bein' in the mountains too long'd turned yer into such a crazy wild coot, even the grizzlies are afeard of yer, an' that y'only come down to rob an' thieve from decent law-abiding citizens once in a while," she said. "You did ask, Mister."

In a second he'd whipped out an old Dance .44 from a pocket and blasted a hole in the ceiling. When the dust and wood chips had settled on the goods, the customers, the shopkeeper and floor, he snatched the pipe off an old timer and threw it out the open door.

"I hate those stinkin' things!" he roared. "Get rid of 'em!"

That shut them all up all right.

Half a dozen pipes flew out the door.

"You behind there," he growled at the storekeeper, "Here's my list, get them mules loaded up double-quick. Be sure to pack them bags same weight either side or I'll be back in here agin sooner than yer'd like."

He waved the pistol in the shopkeepers face with a look so crazy it seemed he might shoot any second.

Then he lowered his piece and gave the quaking man the scrap of paper with his requisites written down on it in a large but tidy hand.

"Don't you want the money from the till and safe?" whispered the storekeeper timidly.

"I ain't no thief," said Briggs. "Take them pelts. I've got sixteen beaver, four elk, two cougar, and a wolverine. On my mules out there."

"We don't take no pelts here," said the storekeeper.

40

BOK! went the .44 into the roof again.

Soon the pelts had been piled in a corner of the store and the shopkeeper, assisted by several of his customers, had carefully packed the provisions, several hundred pounds weight of them, into the big canvas bags on either side of the mules. Flour, beans, bacon, sugar, coffee, black-powder, bird-shot, buckshot, mini-balls, percussion caps, gun-oil, twine, thread, needles, matches, lamp-oil and so on, all went into those capacious bags. Also, tellingly, there were candy-canes, beads, fine cotton-cloth and a mirror; tobacco too, but not for himself.

On his way out he knocked over the skillets again, and a shiny tin coffee pot. He picked them up, looked them over thoughtfully, cradled them in his arms and strode out.

On the porch he stopped, turned, and tipped his hat to O'Halloran.

"Mighty obliged," he growled. "If anyone wants to find me, come up to yonder woods, side o' Snowy Mountain – that's where I'll be."

He pointed at a distant mountain with snow still lingering on its slopes. It looked close enough, but its real distance from the settlement was thirty miles or more.

And with that he swung himself into his saddle and trotted off, the string of mules plodding along gamely behind him, as he whistled happily to himself, not in the least bit concerned about what any white man or women might think of him.

# CHAPTER TWO:
## STRANGERS ON THE TRAIL

After he made camp that night, a few minutes before dark, Briggs was surprised to hear the clink of metal-shod horses plodding along the trail he'd just been walking.

He slipped his rifle out of its case and laid it across his knees. A quick examination of his Dance showed all the caps were clean, the cylinder running free and the hammer free of grit. He put it back in his pocket.

Still spooning his beans, content in front of his fire, he kept a cautious eye on the trail, till three men on weary horses came walking almost up to his fire. His own horse and mules were secured behind him, the saddle bags and packs stored safely under a waterproof tarpaulin for the night.

"Howdy," said the scruffiest, ugliest, dirtiest rider he had ever seen, "You alone, pard?" The man had a greasy, crumpled hat and sweat-stained red bandanna at his throat. He already had a hand on his Colt.

"Nope," said Briggs tersely, wishing his pistol was already in his hand.

"Uh-huh," said the rider, looking around, grinning with the few remaining yellow teeth he had left. He was not an old man, but he may as well have been for all the care he'd taken of himself.

"What ye'got in that stack, Mister?" said a younger but equally unkempt man with holes all over his clothes. He was riding a fine black horse that looked far too good for him, and a gray hat that looked like new. His hand was resting on the

42

shiny stock of a Winchester slung in its boot next to his right leg.

Briggs thought it highly dubious the fellow had come by those expensive items honestly.

"None o' yer business," he said tetchily. "Now ride on, boys, this is my camp an' I ain't lookin' fer comp'ny."

The three men made no movement, showed no inclination to be moving on. They exchanged sly looks with one another. Presently, the third man, a hollow-cheeked, straw-haired scarecrow with no hat, walked his nag round the back of Briggs. He slid down from the saddle and shouted to his fellows:

"Only see one saddle," said the Scarecrow. "Reckon he's alone. Bin' carryin' somethin' good, an' put it in that thar stack."

Briggs went for his rifle but straw-head behind him kicked it away. He felt a pistol poking his temple and decided, wisely, not to draw.

"Whooa mister! Yer mighty touchy ain't yer?" said the Scarecrow, frisking Briggs and helping himself to his Dance pistol and hunting knife. He continued his search for more weapons and removed a second, smaller knife from his boot.

"Spectin' trouble?" said the first rider, now dismounted. A jet of brown tobacco-colored spittle squirted out from between his yellow teeth and hissed as it hit the fire. "Waal, you got it now, mister! We comes into yer camp, friendly as yer like, an' first yer spins us lies, then yer start reachin' fer yer irons like we's Injuns, or outlaws, or somethin'."

The second rider, Holy-Clothes, who'd got down and

flung open the tarpaulin, cackled with laughter.

"Outlaws!" he scoffed, "Outlaws! Ain't no *laws* round these parts to be *out* of, jus' a few savages an' this-here lyin' toad."

"Yeah, Mister," said Yellow-Teeth, helping himself to a handful of the candy-canes, "Why'd yer lie to us? Got somethin' agin us? Huh?"

He walked over to Briggs and bent down so that their noses were almost touching. The man's breath was foul and stinking, as rotten as his soul. His eyes were bloodshot and unhealthy. There were pieces of his breakfast and past meals in his filthy mustache and beard.

"My, yer a big one, ain't yer?" he sneered. "An' that coat, mister – that buffalo? Or bear, maybe?"

"Grizzly," said Briggs. "Come into my camp and helped hisself to my goods."

"Killed him, did ya?" said Yellow-Teeth, "then skinned him?"

"Not me," said Briggs. "My woman done it."

"Yer woman killed him, did she?" said Yellow-Teeth sarcastically, "with a kitchen knife, mebbe, or a hat-pin I'm thinkin'."

The three intruders all cackled and hooted and doubled up with raucous laughter for a while.

The mountain man waited for them to simmer down.

"Nope," he said, "With a six-gauge and buckshot, seein' as yer asked. Took its head clean off."

The three men stopped laughing abruptly.

"Oh, so yer hev a woman, do yer, big feller?" said the

Scarecrow, suddenly interested, taking a seat beside the fire. "Would she be, by any chance, a dirty squaw-woman, mebbe filched from one o' these tribes round hereabouts?"

"She is a squaw-woman at that," said Briggs, "but she ain't dirty, an I didn't filch her from nowhere. She cost me two rifles an' a hundred mini-balls. She's purty as a picture and fierce as a wildcat."

"Uh-huh, is she now, grizzly-man," said Scarecrow, so tell us, where's this purty squaw-woman now? Mebbe you'd like ter introduce us? Would ya? Huh?"

Briggs looked at the hollow-cheeked mask of the Scarecrow, the anger seething inside him, then at Holy-Clothes, and finally Yellow-Teeth. The sun had gone down behind the top of the mountains by now, and the long, dark shadows had merged into one big wall of darkness around them. The flickering fire illuminated the four of them, and the mountain man sighed, and wondered how long it would be before they tried to kill him.

"I asked you a question, you simpleton," said Yellow-Teeth, a rising menace in his voice.

"Yeah," said Holy-Clothes, tilting back his fine gray hat, to reveal his bare, scarred, scalped head that, though healed some time ago, shone white and hideous in the firelight, "You're mighty rude, grizzly-man, an' mebbe I don't care ter share this nice warm fire with a squaw-lover much longer. So's I were you, I'd answer his goddamn question."

"Waal," said the mountain man, "bein' as yer so interested in my woman, guess I'll tell yer. See, she likes ter tag along o' me most the time, but since this here grizzly

45

came at us, she shuns the fire-side. Makes her kinda nervous."

"So she's home in her lil' ol' tee-pee, givin' her titty to them ugly lil' half-breed kids o'yorn?" said Scarecrow. "Thas what yor sayin'?"

"Nope," said Briggs wiping his nose with the back of his hand, "I didn't say that. Wild critters comin' into camp makes her nervous, so soon's it gets dark she likes ter sleep up a tree, in a sort o' hummock she made from a blanket. Sleeps up thar wi' her six-gauge in her lap."

For the first time a look of unease passed between the faces of Yellow-Teeth, Holy-Clothes and Scarecrow. Their eyes narrowed as they tried to work out the full implications of the words of the man in the grizzly-skin coat.

"You're fuller crap, mister," said Yellow-Teeth nastily.

But despite the man's defiant words, Briggs could see his eyes peering up into the trees. His friends were doing the same.

"He's jus' tryin' to get us windy!" said Scarecrow. "Anyhow, ain't no such thing as a goddamn six-gauge!"

"Is too," said Briggs, "Them's English-made for protectin' mail-coaches and such. They take ten drams of powder, three ounce of buckshot, an' a handful o' nails!"

Suddenly, Holy-Clothes leapt to his feet and started blazing off shots from his pistol into the canopy of branches somewhere above the fire.

"Hot-damn!" he yelled, "I see'd sumthin'. It's that squaw woman up' bove our hids! I see'd her, goddammit!"

The other two were on their feet after the very first shot, guns drawn, jumping around like mad-men, pointing and staring into the shadowy trees, letting off shots at something, or nothing, as the fire's flickering changed the shapes of the shadows over their heads.

Bok! Bok! Bok! went their guns, as they danced around like crazy, pointing up at the sky.

Then, remembering their prisoner, they all turned angrily to him, only to find he was grinning at them, his white teeth and laughter-lines showing up clearly in the firelight.

The three pointed their guns towards him, curses rending the air as they took aim, careful to shoot the big man in a vital spot.

There was a fearful, deafening crash of a big-bore gun from somewhere out in the darkness. Scarecrow and Holy Clothes simply disappeared, hit by a wall of lead and sent spinning off into the night. They were dead before they touched the leafy ground. When Yellow-Teeth recovered from the shock of the gun's roar and seeing his two pards knocked down like a pair of rabbits, he turned once again to Briggs and fired.

But Briggs wasn't there. The shot ricocheted off the tree-trunk he'd been leaning against a moment before. How could a big man move so quickly? More importantly, where was he now? And where was his squaw? Yellow-Teeth, real name Carlton Earl Tomkins, wanted for murder in Wyoming and Idaho as it happened, now had a dilemma. Stay by the fire and he would surely be shot or picked off by the giant or his squaw. Move away from it, and he would be plunged into the terrible darkness, with death perhaps coming like a faceless black shadow to take him, horribly, to the very depths of hell.

He licked his lips, frozen to the spot for a moment, desperately thinking what to do. Then it came to him: his horse. He'd make a dash for it and go for broke. His horse – or one of the others, for all three were still saddled – would take him away to safety, and he could then decide how to get his revenge.

He glanced at the fire – a mistake, for he lost whatever small degree of night vision he had – and bolted for the horses. He ran smack into the neck of the big black gelding that Scarecrow had taken off a fat rancher (who now, of course, no longer needed it) so that he got a mouthful of horsehair. He groped around, and in a couple of hops and he was up on its back, leaning forward for the reins, his legs kicking furiously to spur the horse forward.

But that was as far as he got. He was kicking, but not connecting with the horse's sides; and the reason was simple. Somebody had grabbed him by the small of his back and lifted him bodily into the air. That same person now threw him straight into a tree-trunk, at which point he dropped his Colt into the darkness. By the time he'd recovered himself a little, crawling around in the gloom, small strong hands had grasped his hair and nicked his scalp three parts round his skull and was already removing his hair. His screams rent the darkness, but the mountain man's squaw-wife on his back was unmoved.

"Wait, my dear," said Briggs, "he ain't quite dead yet, don't yer know it's rude to whip off a feller's hair when he's still alive?"

He had the bad habit of talking to Kana-ha, his wife, in

48

English, when he knew perfectly well how to speak her own Wynoochee tongue. The funny thing was, she guessed his meaning, and quit removing the hair while she rode the killer's back as if he were a pony, and gave him a quick, deep slit to the throat. Of course, she had to leap clear at this point, to avoid getting blood on her clothes or moccasins.

The mountain man threw a bundle of fine twigs on the fire, and the camp was soon illuminated by bright flames, revealing the outcome of the fight. Two men peppered with buckshot lay to one side of the fire, and the third sprawled on the other side, twitching, in an ever-widening pool of blood, next to the pile of provisions.

Kana-ha, meaning 'Mountain Bird' in her native tongue, deftly removed Yellow-Teeth's scalp; then Scarecrow's long, yellow hair.

"Narwah," she remarked, meaning 'filthy'.

Then she examined Holy Clothes' bare head and cursed.

"Yer daddy got him first, I reck'n," said Briggs, then said the same in Wynoochee, which made her shriek with laughter.

He asked her why she was always so keen to take the scalps of white men, since it was a horrible, heathen custom. She replied that it was revenge for all the members of her tribe, and other tribes, killed by the white men. Besides, if he wouldn't do it, somebody had to do it for him; it showed the camp whose side he was really on, and earned him respect!

They continued speaking in her language for a while.

"They will only stop killing us when we're all dead," she told him.

"Not if I can help it," said Briggs; "I'd kill the lot of them and give the land back to the Red Man if I could."

"But then," she said sadly, "we wouldn't be able to get any more bacon or cotton-cloth, or shot and powder for my gun."

Briggs looked at his wife with admiration and wonder for a moment. He loved every word she spoke, every movement of her body, every expression of her beautiful face. Well worth the two rifles and hundred bullets, he mused.

"Anyways," said Briggs, returning to English again, "we got three fine horses, a load o' guns an' ammo to trade. Likely they'll have stolen money I can spend later, too. I'll keep the Winchester – always wanted one o' them things. Now we jus' need to tend to them horses, an' I'll drag this scum out of our sight so's we can get some sleep. Then, woman, you can sleep down here with me tonight. That's an order."

He repeated these last commands in her own tongue, and she laughed, helped him lug the bodies away from the fire; but after she'd reloaded the single big barrel of her old six-gauge, not forgetting to replace the old percussion cap, she climbed back to her hammock high above the fire, and settled down with the gun in her lap once more.

"Pah," said Briggs to himself, "What use is a woman if she sleeps up a tree every night like that?"

But he already knew the answer to that one.

# CHAPTER THREE:
## AMONG THE WYNOOCHEE

After arriving at the Wynoochee camp, which was judiciously located on a plateau part-way up a mountain, the first task was to offer tribute to the chief, a wise old fellow named Fire-Cloud, who was never quite sure he had made the right decision letting the big white man pitch a tepee on the edge of his village. In the countryside around the Snowy Mountain, called 'Channashi-Saqua' in Wynoochee, pioneers and prospectors were claiming tracts of lands for themselves, pitching their tents, then putting up log cabins, corrals, boundary markers, fences. These settlers and miners were in the habit of calling on the Army to protect them whenever Indians, friendly or otherwise, turned up anywhere nearby. Many were in the habit of loosing off shots at Indians on sight.

Therefore, the Wynoochee kept away from the whites. Ever since the wars of the 1850's, they knew that to resist the hordes of settlers brought swift retribution in the form of attacks from mounted soldiers, whose leaders were only too happy to flatten the few remaining Indian camps.

Fire-Cloud still viewed Briggs with suspicion, but soon that doubt as to whether the white man would one day betray them would be allayed for good. In the meantime, many fine gifts kept him content but watchful, biding his time. After Briggs latest journey, two of the bushwhacker's rifles, good war-issue springfields, and a quantity of ammunition were taken to him. The goods were accepted with only a grunt of approval, but Briggs knew how much such weapons were prized by Wynoochee warriors.

Briggs kept his newly acquired Winchester hidden for now, since the chief's appreciation of his own guns would likely diminish at the sight of it.

Paying homage to the chief was one thing, but Briggs knew better than simply to give away items to his other neighbors. While Wynoochee braves and women might readily accept free knives, rifles, utensils, trinkets and so on from him, they would nevertheless despise him for handing out goods for no obvious reason. While sharing food was the norm, charitable giving of valuable items, except to a close family member, was considered a weakness on the part of the giver. Trade was the correct way to do things. A good metal pan was worth two beaver's pelts; a small flask of gunpowder equalled two beaver or one antelope's skin; a good rifle might fetch ten beaver or two buffalo skins and so on. The main thing was, Briggs knew, to ask the same amount for the same item to each of his neighbors; otherwise there would be sullen resentment and bad blood towards not only himself, but also the man who acquired his goods 'cheaply.' Fair and consistent trading was essential when dealing with Indians, who had strong notions of how much any commodity or artefact was worth.

There were, however, curious distortions in the Wynoochee system of values. For example, a small string of cheap glass beads might be swapped for a class one bear-skin, or a high quality tomahawk that had taken a craftsman a whole week to make. And, as Briggs knew only too well, and to his delight, a pretty Wynoochee girl might be handed over as a bride by her father for only two used rifles, a keg of powder and a hundred mini-balls.

This kind of 'marriage trade,' however, was concluded only if the father trusted the groom, who had to accept the life-long obligations upon joining a large, extended family. These family members (that an outsider would not even know were related to his bride before the marriage) might then begin to give the newlyweds venison, antelope or buffalo meat, or salmon when they least expected it, or invite them to share in a meal or feast for any of a hundred reasons. The husband would be expected to divide the proceeds of his own hunts with them. If the favor were not returned, despite a man being fit and able to hunt, then his share of relative's hunts might grow tiny, or dry up entirely.

In times of dearth, however, hunters would never think of leaving a relative or even a neighbor in desperate need of food. In the genial community of a Wynoochee tribe, the tradition was that food should reach every member of the camp, especially in late winter and early spring, when stocks of preserved goods ran low, and the products of hunting and fishing were most needed.

Cooking, food preparation and its proper preservation and storing were performed by Wynoochee women. Once, Kana-Ha had tried to beat Briggs with a hazel broom after he put food into a pot and tried to cook it over a fire by their tepee.

"Am I too lazy and stupid to cook and provide food for my family?" she screamed in front of their neighbors. "You shame me by doing woman's work where everyone can see you! Do you intend also to sew clothes and scrape hides and tend to our children so that I grow idle and fat, and everybody points at us and laughs?"

At this point he had to give her a gentle smack or two on the rump to re-assert his dominance, thus emulating the behavior of his neighbors in a domestic quarrel; subsequently Kana-Ha was left to do the domestic work, while he cleaned his guns, sharpened blades, ate, drank, and prepared himself for expeditions out onto the mountains or whatever. Thus was matrimonial harmony restored, much to the approval of all, especially the wronged lady herself. For, though she might go on hunting and trading trips with her man, activities never before undertaken by Wynoochee females, she had no intention whatever of letting Briggs usurp any of her own wifely tasks.

What did come into a husband's duties, however, was teaching his two fine boys of five and eight years some of the manly, warrior skills they would later need, namely, the riding of ponies, using a bow and arrows, basic fighting and wrestling skills, swimming in the river and, eventually, proficient use of firearms. Already they accompanied him on bird, squirrel or rabbit hunting day-trips into the hills or forest; but on longer forays, while his wife went with him, all four children were sent to the tepee of Kana-Ha's parents.

Like all grandparents, this couple, not elderly at only forty-five or so, doted on their charges, taking delight at teaching them the wisdom, lore and skills required of their people. For girls these included food gathering and preservation, cooking, sewing, weaving, curing hides and gathering firewood. The work might go on from after breakfast until the sun went down. The remedy for sore muscles or aching fingers was more work; and while laughing and joking, story-telling and the singing of songs might fill the air, the toil was relentless.

Both boys and girls were schooled in tepee construction, the making and using of tools from bone, antler and flint, and the artistic skills of painting fabulous designs of animal, bird, tree, plant or flower on just about anything with a flat surface (including humans and horses).

Throughout the processes of labor, the adults passed on traditional stories, tribal laws and customs, and their wisdom of spiritual things such as the worship of spirits, and the Great Spirit in particular, who was the creator and supreme being of this world and the next.

Seeing all this going on, Briggs himself was careful not to over-indulge his offspring. He was kind, fair and firm with them at all times. Life in Indian camps was hard but bearable, requiring a sort of iron self-discipline, even for children. For example, when gathering nuts or berries in autumn, no person was allowed to eat even one, however hungry they were, until the evening when the spoils were shared out amongst the various families who did the picking. Similarly, when drying or smoking fish and meat on racks over fires, and later in the cooking process, woe betide the person who took even a morsel before the final share-out. And when children were sent out to watch over the grazing horses, each had only a few small pieces of flat corn-bread to eat and a skin bag of water that sufficed for a watch of up to twelve hours, or whenever the horses were brought back down to the village. Only then did the whole camp eat their evening meal.

Boys, from the age of about thirteen, joined their fathers on hunting or raiding expeditions. Then, they shared the hardships and dangers of the men, and it was common for boys to be injured or even killed from any one of a multitude of dangers, the most common one being riding accidents. Indian men made wonderful riders, but the skill was hard-earned from practice and many, many falls.

Briggs noted that Indian fathers were not over-demonstrative in showing affection to their male offspring, especially in public, and he refrained from doing so himself, so as not to embarrass them in front of their peers. All four of his children (girls of three and seven, boys of five and eight) were taller than full-blooded Indian children of their own ages, but luckily all had the dark eyes and olive skin of their mother. They were beautiful, wonderfully athletic and smart as whips. Briggs was as proud of his family as a father could be, counting himself lucky that his children were being brought up in Wynoochee society. His observations had long convinced him of the superiority of the natives' way of life, the way they lived in and alongside the natural world, rather than try to bend it to their will, as was the habit of the white race.

As for his wife, she was something of a rebel amongst her own people. Not best-pleased at being traded for guns and given to a white man, after the wedding ceremony, she refused point-blank to leave the tribe to go with him.

Bemused by the young squaw's attitude, Briggs asked Fire-Cloud if they might stay in camp, and was given a tepee – for the right trades, of course. Thereafter, he made the Indian village his home, moving whenever the elders decided to strike camp, and helping re-construct the tepees, fire-pits, pelt-drying frames and so on when the tribe reached its new location. Soon he was invited on the deer hunts, fishing expeditions and even a raid to steal ponies from their arch-enemies, the Yakima.

During a Yakima raid on their own camp, he was appalled to see the use old Fire-Cloud made of the tribe's women. When about a hundred Yakima braves rode into the village one dawn, attempting to drive away all the mounts, he was shocked to see the women as well as men run out into the midst of their enemy. By the time a half-dressed Briggs had gathered his rifle and ammunition, Kana-Ha and about thirty other women and girls were already fetching horses from their tethering lines to their men. Others were attaching long, low ropes between trees on the fringes of the village to form trip-wires to unhorse their enemies. While the Wynoochee riders knew the tripping points and rode round them, many of the Yakimas were thrown from their horses and despatched on the ground with tomahawk, knife or war-club, some of them wielded by women. Other Yakima were killed by rifle fire, the camp having an abundance of firearms, thanks largely to those brought in and traded by Briggs. Even without guns, the Wynoochee were one the most formidable fighting tribes of the north-west, being themselves war-like, fearless and artful in the use of gun, war-bow, lance and

57

hatchet.

The simple expedient of firmly tethering the ponies close by the village largely prevented their mounts being run off that day. Being avid raiders of horses themselves, they knew better than to leave them in a grazing herd at night. Furthermore, they had, like all Indian settlements, a counter-measure to fight off a raiding party. It was a habit of Wynoochee men to talk long and in detail of past battles and raids, and discuss at length how they would fight their next one, be it an expedition far away in another tribe's territory, or a defensive action at their own camp. Thus, while Briggs had stood his ground and blasted several Yakima from their mounts, his Indian comrades soon went over to the attack. They pursued the would-be raiders far into the hills and into the prairies below, killing many of their enemy in the process.

As he was told by one of his brother-in-laws, Nar-Ki-Sarwak (literally 'He-Who-Catches-Eagles') at the celebratory feast:

"It is not good for a Yakima from the low lands to come looking for blood and ponies in these hills. Every few years they have tried, and then they forget, and try again. The result is always the same. The Yakima are as the coyote, the owl or the fox, to be feared only by children; but the Wynoochee are as the bull-buffalo, the cougar and the grizzly, that when wounded grow ever stronger and more fearsome."

It had also been well noted in the battle that the white man, shirtless, shoeless, in only his long-johns, had stood his ground in the camp, slaying many Yakima, and frightening a good few others with both the blasts of his gun and fearsome growls and cusses at the war-painted interlopers.

And when the old Chief Fire-Cloud spoke up at the banquet, there was a silencing of the drums, the laughter and the stories as he turned to Briggs and said:

"You have fought well, Wa-Ki-Chichna, and shown great courage. But when the white soldiers with their rifles and long knives come, will you again stand side by side with your Wynoochee brothers, and once more fight like the bear that is wounded by an arrow?"

"I will, my chief," he said in their own tongue, "I will fight for my wife, my children, and for my brothers here. And I will die too, if I have to, and take as many of them down as I can, before the eagle-bird of the Great Spirit comes calling for me."

There was much cheering and praising of these words, but the chief held up his hand for silence again.

"But why is it that you have come to live amongst us, and are prepared to fight the army of the whites? Are they still not your tribe, your own blood-brothers? How do we know you will not change your mind and fight against us when the time comes?"

"Now hear me, men of the Wynoochee," said Briggs, "and hear me good. Since you have asked me, I will tell you my whole story, that I have uttered to no man since I left the east. Then you can be sure I stand with you, and that although my skin is white, my heart is now Wynoochee like your own. You need to know first, that I fought in a war where as many whites were slain as stars in the sky."

"We have heard of this war," said the Chief, "when white killed white, and regret that any of the soldiers survived at all; but how is it that so many died and yet still they come, as many in number as the buffalo that once crossed the plains, to usurp our land and kill our people?"

"That," said Briggs, choosing his words carefully, "is because great war-canoes taller than any tepee, each one made of hundreds of trees, arrive each day with thousands more of my kind. Each vessel carries as many whites as people in this village. You are right to live here in these mountains and defend them with your lives. If you continue to do this, you will have a chance to survive, while other tribes have almost disappeared."

A gloomy silence came over the previously joyful feast, as the warriors took all this in; it was not what they wanted to hear; but no man questioned the wisdom of his words, for they had heard similar things before from braves from other tribes who had traveled into the lands already conquered by the whites.

At last the old Chief spoke up again.

"And now I repeat my question," he said. "You, with your bear-skin and rifle, how do we know you will fight these blue soldiers if you fought in their great army before? Are you not of their blood?"

"No," said Briggs, "I am not. Let me continue with my story. The white soldiers fought against each other in two great armies, as I have said. One army wore dark blue, and came from the north. This is the one that threatens you today. The other one, from the south, wore clothes of gray, or

60

sometimes brown, and were the sworn enemies of the blue. I lived in the south, but I did not wish to fight, and at first both armies left me alone and the war seemed far away."

He paused, looked about him at the Indian faces caught in the firelight, and wished he had not been asked these difficult questions, since he found it painful to continue.

"How then," said the Chief, "did you come to join in this great war of the whites? Tell us, white man, for we wish to know these things."

There was another silence while Briggs thought how best to explain himself. The braves had gathered close about him, seated cross-legged, whispering to each other. The fire grew brighter, illuminating Briggs face a little better, and the braves were astonished to see tears trickling down the cheeks of the white giant. Presently, he said:

"I was a farmer from the land of the gray tribe. My neighbors said the blue soldiers would come to take my cows and horses, maybe to kill me, but I did not believe them. One day, when I was in a field working, they did come. They stole my horses, my cows, my money, guns, everything. And my wife – they raped her and killed her, and burned down my house with my children inside."

There was a murmur of horror from even these most hardened warriors, who had, in their time, themselves seen most kinds of atrocity carried out in warfare.

"So," said Briggs, "with great hatred in my heart, I joined the army of the gray tribe against the blue. As a young man I had once been trained in the ways of war. So they gave me a sword, and put me in charge of a hundred mounted men. Our

61

great war-chief was called Robert E. Lee and he led us to victory after victory. He had a gray beard and a gray war-horse and was a leader like no other. But the more we killed, the more there came to fight us, while all the time we grew fewer. Their guns were better, they had warm tepees and blankets, and much food, while we were cold and starving and often ran out of ammunition. Before the end there was a battle in a place called Gettysburg that covered many hills and valleys, and we fought for three days. Finally, our chief made a grave mistake and sent us out into the open, where the enemy's guns cut us down. We fell, and lay like leaves after the first frost. Many of my friends were killed. Some of us rode away, and though we fought again, the blue soldiers soon conquered all of my land. Many like me, escaped and came west. I suppose that now another man, perhaps one from that blue army, occupies my farm; but I never cared to go back and find out. Those I had loved were gone, and without the killing of my enemies to keep me busy, I grew desperate, and traveled from place to place."

Here he paused and glanced around to see if he had the tribe's attention. He needn't have worried on that score; every pair of eyes was fixed firmly on him.

"I came out here," he said, "to the land of the Wynoochee, trying to forget all I had seen and known. I did not intend to start again, but when I saw Kana-Ha I knew she could give me children, and help me heal, take away my sorrow. Now that I have a family that gives purpose to my life, like you, I will do anything to protect them. Therefore, I tell you this: I swear on the lives of my four children, that if the blue soldiers ever come into these hills, I will fight with you against them, on this you may depend, my Wynoochee brothers. And when the bullets sing and the long-knives flash, I shall fight and die as one of you. All I ask of you is that, if I am cut down, to see that my wife and children do not starve."

He looked around at the sympathetic faces of the men, who were now murmuring to each other, well satisfied with the story they had just heard, then turned to their leader, saying:

"Does that answer your question, Chief Fire-Cloud?"

But there was no direct reply from any of the warriors gathered there, for none was necessary, only looks of wonder at this man, who fought and feasted and dwelt amongst them, speaking their language almost as cleverly as a chief or medicine man.

From that night onward Briggs, in the eyes of his formerly suspicious neighbors, became an accepted member of the tribe, a white Wynoochee; for it was obvious to them now, that he shared not only their camp, their food, their way of life, but also their stubborn, resolve to make a last stand against hopeless odds.

# CHAPTER FOUR:
## ATTACK ON SNOWY MOUNTAIN

Somewhere down in the valley they fought. It was one of the very last actions of the Indian wars, not a battle, but a skirmish.

Five companies of cavalry totalling five hundred and fifty-seven men began by attacking a mere fifteen braves in a hunting party. But the fifteen soon became over three hundred warriors on ponies. Soon, it was not clear who was the pursuer and who the pursued. There were shots fired, shouting, horses falling, and men crying out in pain as they were struck. The woodlands of tall redwoods, spruce and cedar that covered the mountain-sides, well-known to the Indians, became a place of terror and confusion to the attackers.

Though only a handful of men were killed on each side, a great many were wounded, most of them soldiers. Eventually the bugles signaled 'retreat', and the troopers withdrew in some disorder. The soldiers were pursued, harried, and in fact, defeated.

Though it was a senseless conflict in that it had no real objective on the part of the aggressors, and was begun without provocation, it nevertheless had a decisive result: the Snowy Mountain remained in tribal hands.

Neither history books nor regimental records give a reason why, on that day of 15 July, 1875, the army attacked at all. It is only recorded that troopers passing through heavy forest in a mountain valley chased a group of braves and soon discovered a large 'hostile' camp located on a plateau; and that, as they investigated, they were turned away from the heights in a hail of lead and arrows.

Or, as one senior officer's report stated: 'We were obliged to withdraw in an orderly manner'.

That is one way of putting it.

Why exactly the cavalry were patrolling there in such numbers has never been explained; most likely their officers suspected the mountains were home to Indians camps as yet unbroken by defeat, and were spoiling for a fight. In any event, they were at least successful in finding out two things. Firstly, that the heavily forested mountain slopes were inhospitable and eminently unsuitable for occupation by settlers. And secondly, the current inhabitants had no intention of giving them up anytime soon.

And so they had fought.

It is recorded in troopers' letters that a tall, black-bearded white man in a bear-skin coat fought on the side of the Wynoochee. They said he stood, immovable, in the path of a cavalry charge. The sight of a crazy, wild-looking man of the woods also gave rise to many rumors and stories told in the mess-halls, barracks and camps in later years.

Most of them concurred that the bearded man was knocked off his feet four times by Army bullets, and four times he got up again and resumed firing his repeating rifle. They say also that he made no attempt to conceal himself, blocking the way forward with his body, unheeding of both the bullets, and later, his wounds. Then, as the soldiers withdrew in disarray after finding themselves outflanked, he is said to have picked up an unhorsed trooper who was about to be scalped, thrown him back on a loose horse, and sent him scampering home like a frightened child that had seen a ghost.

"Who the hell *are* you?" quaked the soldier, as he was bodily picked up by the bear-like apparition covered in blood.

"One o' them as already owns the goddamn mountain!" was the legendary refrain.

# EPILOGUE: HOMESTEADERS

The attack on the Snowy Mountain was never repeated. The reasons for this were threefold.

Firstly, local politicians and Army leaders were extremely reluctant to get embroiled in a dispute with a *white* settler on the mountain, the very people they were sent to protect, and secondly, as at least one white man was living there, they could not argue that non-natives were under threat. Thirdly, in order to save face, the senior officers wrote reports suggesting they had dealt the 'hostiles' a severe blow and disengaged at leisure. Thus the Wynoochee were left in possession of several thousand acres of mountain country, which, through rumor and exaggeration, soon gained a fearful reputation as the haunt of savage tribes. To this day the nearby farmers and ranchers still call the Snowy Mountain area the 'Skeleton Hills' because of the number of human remains found thereabouts.

But these were not the bones of slaughtered travelers or pioneers.

Fire-Cloud, along with many of his tribe, died soon after the Army incursion, when small-pox swept through the region's Native Americans in the late 1870's. The reality was that so many perished, that it was impossible to bury all the dead. Many bodies were simply taken out onto the mountainside and left there for the wild animals. Nor was this the only epidemic to decimate the inhabitants. It is not known by what means these diseases reached the Snowy Mountain, perhaps through contact with white traders, or other tribes already infected. At any rate, these tragedies caused the Wynoochee population to plummet.

Fifteen or so years later, in 1889, a gray-haired man called Briggs traveled to the regional land office near present day Seattle to register five claims, under the Homestead Act of 1862, one for himself, and one for each of four family members. He also filed claims for five Native Americans. A young lawyer called MacAvoy was employed to ease the process. While the Briggs family claims were successful, only two of the native ones were approved, after an inspection by a Land Officer. The criteria for occupying and owning the plots included marking boundaries, building a twelve by fourteen foot log cabin or lodge, 'improving' the land by clearing scrub, and engaging in farming or other agricultural or ranching activity, as well as eventually paying $1.25 per acre to secure full ownership.

There is a clause which prohibits the granting of homesteads to those who had fought or opposed the United States government with armed force, but due to the long passage of time that had elapsed, or perhaps the paying of a bribe, or, more likely still, the lack of official documentation on the subject, past conflicts were conveniently overlooked. That Briggs had been a Confederate officer would not have disqualified him from his claim, the law having been changed in 1867 to allow 'gentlemen of the south' to file; and, in any case, he had not revealed his former allegiance to the Confederacy to anyone other than his Indian allies.

Though it is a mystery as to where the money for the six

claims came from, it seems likely the sale of surplus horses and ponies to homesteaders, miners and others in need of them paid for the land.

The seven claims gave Briggs, his family and the others control of the plateau, and the only good access route up to it from the valleys below, thus making it impossible for outsiders to buy up the forested or rock-strewn land at higher elevations; in any case, there was no living to be had there. It eventually became part of a National Park.

The Briggs Ranch remains, one of several in the region still owned by descendants of Native Americans. The raising and training of horses remains the most important local source of income.

Though the once great Wynoochee tribe may officially be extinct, unrecognized, its customs largely forgotten, its blood-lines merged with other tribes and peoples, it is nevertheless true that a few of its descendants persist, guardian-possessors of the great Snowy Mountain, undefeated to the present day.

On the main trail up to the plateau a hand-painted sign reads:

**'No Hunting. No hiking. No Way Through.'**

And it would be a very foolish traveler indeed that didn't take the hint.

## THE END

# BOOK THREE...

# WARPATHS AND PEACEMAKERS

*'I hate all white people. You are thieves and liars. You have taken away our land and made us outcasts.'*
Chief Sitting Bull, 1883

# WARPATHS AND PEACEMAKERS

## CHAPTER ONE:
## THOU SHALT NOT STEAL

**Somewhere in the heavily wooded hills that fringe Bull Moose Mountain, a place on the frontier so far west that if you went much further you'd fall into the Pacific Ocean itself, old Sam Jordan was leading his two mules along a narrow track.**

He had chosen to trap here because it was one of the few places left where pelts were still to be had in any quantity. Furthermore, a recent rise in prices had motivated him to try his luck for one more season. Then he would finally count up his considerable earnings and go to see his daughter near Spokane. There, his son-in-law had built Sam Jordan a fine log cabin on the farm, not least because the spread had been bankrolled by half a century's trapping.

Trapping had been a lucrative occupation for the bold and skilful man; but now the trade was coming to an end. Beaver were scarce most places, and fashions had changed. To Jordan's disgust, trading posts were paying less for good skins now than twenty years ago. There was one exception, that of good quality big-cat skins, which still sold for a premium. These would eventually find their way to New York, Washington, Europe or whatever, to become high quality items of clothing, status symbols reserved for the very richest members of society.

A disturbance in the vegetation just ahead of Jordan caught his attention. There were shreds of bark scratched from the still leafless sapling poles, and bare patches of earth where the leaf-mold had been disturbed. About ten paces further on, he found the cause. Neatly snared round its neck, a large lynx lay dead, the fine condition of its pelt, and the clarity of its eyes indicating that it had been there but a few hours. The snare was still attached to its 'drag', a large piece of fallen tree-trunk which, despite its bulk, had nevertheless been pulled along the ten yards or so before the beast succumbed.

Soothing his now nervous beasts of burden, which had spooked at scenting the big cat in their path, Jordan edged forward cautiously to take a look. He noted that this method of trapping, a man-made plaited-steel wire, thin but incredibly strong, was typical of the Indians in that area. Snaring was a relatively cheap and effective means of taking animals, allowing a single man multiple chances of a catch, whereas heavier, expensive spring-traps, though more reliable, limited the number of sites that could be made active at any one time. The other advantage of snares was that they seldom damaged the valuable pelts of the quarry – such as this one. Jordan examined the cat. Its fur was very pale, its fine, thick, silver-russet winter-coat being just about the best he'd ever seen.

The North-West Basin Commodities Company, one of many operating on or inland from the Pacific coast of Washington Territory, would, he knew, be even more likely to pay big money for an extra light-colored specimen like this.

Though he had almost a full load of other species sought after by the Company, including three class one bobcat pelts (only a third the size of a lynx) he lacked one of these, and greedily speculated as to how much Dan Hooper would pay him – instead, perhaps, of remembering what the local Wynoochee, Kikiallus, or Wappato Indians did to those helping themselves to their property. Indians, as all white trappers knew, did not take kindly to interference with their own traps or snares. While they would invariably take a white man's catch, trap and all, it was not wise to snatch theirs. The reason for this was that most tribes asserted that a thief could rightfully be killed by the man he stole from. Furthermore, they had legendary powers of tracking down man or beast alike. There was even the case of a trapper being followed over fifty miles and finally being hacked down on the threshold of a fur company post on the outskirts of Seattle.

Jordan was aware of these things; he knew he should have quietly passed the site without so much as a second glance.

But he didn't. Instead he removed the wildcat from the snare, took out his knife and hastily began to remove its skin. It was a risky business, he knew, as he expertly made the nicks and cuts to get the pelt off in one piece so as to secure the best possible price. It was already mid morning, and the true owner of the lynx might be along at any time. Jordan fervently hoped though, the Indian was far away, planning to check his wires in this particular valley another day. Early morning was the best time to do the rounds of traps and snares after all, such quarry being usually caught after its nocturnal or dawn activity.

"Today," thought Jordan, "I'm in luck, I'll have this critter skinned and the pelt rolled and be on my way. I won't stop for a few miles, and I'll walk my mules along a shallow part of the river at the bottom of the valley to throw off any pursuer. Besides, I've always got my guns."

Then, a sudden realisation sent a shiver of fear through the trapper's body. He touched the big, right-side pocket of his jacket. No gun. He remembered with a start that the ancient cap-and-ball Colt Peacemaker was still in a saddle-bag on mule number two, next to his rifle, both weapons wrapped in oiled cloth to keep out the previous day's rain. He looked up from his work, glanced about him, scoured the path back along the hillside. Then he peered to where the track ahead of him disappeared among the trees and vegetation. No sign of man or beast disturbed his vision. And yet the air was still. There were no birds singing or calling anywhere nearby, and that was unusual.

The mules, however, almost always able to sense danger before their driver, were once more relaxed and placid. After smelling the fresh, warm stink of the flayed animal and realizing that the wildcat was dead, they had surmised, perceptive animals that they were, that its uncured pelt was just another item they would have to carry, unpleasant-smelling and heavy as it was.

Laying down his knife, Jordan walked over to the second mule, stopping only to wipe his gory fingers on a low, bushy juniper branch. He located the roll of oiled-cotton cloth that held his rifle, but failed to find the bag containing his pistol.

76

He searched, first slowly and methodically through the saddle–bags and packs, then, impatient to locate the gun, began frantically spilling his blankets, pelts, food items and miscellaneous goods onto the ground.

Cursing, he bent to pick up his chattels, and chanced to look into the undergrowth where something caught his eye. Then he froze. The bag he had sought was hanging on some thorns a few feet away, discarded and empty. At the same time he caught the whiff of cigarette smoke – and turned slowly around. On his other side, a few yards into the woods, sitting on a fallen tree, a large, elderly, bull-necked Indian was watching him intently. The man was dressed in brown buckskin with neat, uniform fringes; his distinctive clothing had white, decorative stitching all over it, with small pictures of beaver, buffalo, moose and deer skilfully painted in white. The old colt pistol was on his lap. A couple of wire snares lay at his feet.

Jordan surveyed the old man's face, trying to discern his intentions, but gleaned nothing from the impassive, coppery features. The native showed neither hostility nor friendliness; but his dark eyes followed and watched the white man as an alert cat might watch a bird hopping around just out of reach.

Sam Jordan edged back towards mule number two. The one with his rifle. The old Indian made no movement, or sign that he might object to him retrieving his gun, until the mountain man's hand touched upon the oil-skin. He had to turn his back on the native man to get the rifle free of its bindings, but as he did so, he heard the hammer of the pistol click back. He turned round ever so slowly. The Indian had him covered.

Though the early spring air was cool, Jordan began to sweat. That the Colt would be left loaded was a given, out in the woods; there was no point carrying a side-arm for personal protection in the wilderness if you left it unloaded. Damp or no damp, if the first chamber did not ignite, well, one of the remaining five surely would. Indians were known to be terrible marksmen with pistols, but, nevertheless, the odds of getting out that rifle and not being shot in the back, or rushed with a knife, were practically nil. So Jordan stepped away from the mules and tried another tactic.

"Hey now, old feller, don't go gettin' the wrong idea now, I's only skinnin' the cat ready fer yer ready ter take – let me finish it an' hand it over to yer. Would yer like me ter do that? Would yer?"

The tiniest flicker of a smile – or perhaps a wince – in the corner of the Indian's face gave Jordan a glimmer of hope.

The Indian puffed at the cigarette, glanced at the lynx, three-parts finished in its preparation, and then at the trembling white man. He said nothing; but Jordan took this as a good sign, went back to the cat and set nervously to the task of completing the job. From time to time he glanced back over his shoulder at the Indian, who was still sitting on the tree-stump, his cigarette finished now, chewing on something, some jerky perhaps, the pistol laid in his lap, but ever watchful of the intruder hard at work on his catch.

Twenty minutes later and Jordan had finished the skinning. He rolled the thing up, and even tied it neatly with a couple of lengths of twine he carried in his pockets. He walked tentatively over to the Indian and tried to present him with the pelt.

"There ye' are," he said, "That'll git yer a fine price down at the Tradin' Post. That's class one, that is, no mistake, glad ter hilp yer out, hey feller, hey?"

As the old Indian made no effort to take the skin, Jordan was left holding it, his voice growing ever more desperate.

"Now don't ye think o' doin' anythin' yer'd regret, now feller," he said, carefully laying down the bundle. "There's a sheriff and a deputy not far from here, an' them men at the Tradin' Post'd not look kindly on yer doin' anythin' yer'd regret, d'yer hear me now feller?"

Jordan backed away slowly towards his mules. But somehow, and it wasn't a prophesy difficult to make, he knew he wasn't going make it back to civilization.

The Indian stood up, and heaved a great sigh.

Still, though, Jordan tried to make his bargain.

"Now, lissen here, feller," he said, "if yer were t'give me that pistol back, I'd be happy ter gi' yer some real fine baccy, an' I got powder, an' a piece o' bacon, an', an'..."

But then his mind went blank. A tear rolled down his cheek.

He tried to think. It was difficult, for always, always, those dark eyes regarded him impassively. There was no hint of a smile now, no sign of what he intended to do.

Finally, the trapper remembered with a start the very thing that had got him out of a couple of tricky situations with the red men before.

"Whiskey!" he said. "I got a lil' whiskey left in my

79

saddle-bag. Ivry-body likes whiskey, I'll git it fer ye if yer'll only-"

He never finished the sentence. At least it was a single, merciful, humane shot, right through the heart, causing the crows and ravens to caw and complain all along the echoing valley.

Some Indians, it turned out, were good shots with a pistol after all.

The old Indian set to work with his own skinning knife and soon had the white man's hide stretched out round the trunk of one of the larger redwoods that fringed the path, neatly pegged with a dozen of the small iron nails he used for pinning his pelts. He was loathe to waste more.

The dreadful corpse and filthy clothes he had cut off prior to the skinning were thrown down into the gorge for the bears and coyotes. As for Jordan's mules and gear, they were forfeited the moment he stepped off the path to touch the lynx.

His skin, however, was now a useful commodity. Left to dry on the tree, it advertised to Indian and white man alike, that those who stole from a Kikiallus would have to face stern consequences.

It was a nice job, too, and not without a bit of humor. The mask of that human pelt, complete with scalp, was carefully preserved. And pinning the eyes to the bark so that they peeked through their correct holes in the flat face was devilishly funny to the Native Men that passed by, at least for a few days, until a raven ate them. Eyes are always the first thing eaten by the crows and ravens, every country dweller knows that.

The word soon spread far and wide amongst the Kikiallus, of how old Johnny One-Pine had served up some strong medicine to a white man, adding to his already considerable fame. For there is nothing an Indian likes more than a tale of retribution against his enemies. And white men would do well to remember that to Native Americans, the taking of revenge is as natural and inevitable as the rising of the sun.

## CHAPTER TWO:
## TROUBLE AT THE TRADING POST

To the Trading Post at Bull Moose Mountain there arrived a man called James O'Rourke, a young talent in the up and coming business of pulp-wood. It was the height of the spring trading in furs, but O'Rourke took no interest in this age-old trade. He represented a paper-making syndicate somewhere back cast, and he sported a brand new tweed outfit of such finery that Daniel Hooper, who was general manager at Bull Moose and could appraise a pelt at a single glance, arched his eyebrows in disapproving surprise when the young fellow sauntered, dandy-like, into his domain.

Nevertheless, Hooper soon made friends with O'Rourke over the counter of the little trading post, and they chatted amicably for a good while. O'Rourke, however, withdrew to the side of the room when each gaunt, pelt-laden Indian crossed the threshold. He seemed slightly nervous each time one of the copper-skinned men appeared, though he watched their actions with great interest.

"So you're James O'Rourke?" said Hooper reminiscently, in a lull from trading, "I got a sort of notion I heard that name before."

O'Rourke nodded languidly and flapped a handkerchief at a large mosquito that was worrying him.

"Maybe you have. I had a grandfather in the same business as yourself, buying furs for the company. His name was James O'Rourke too, though everybody called him Jimmy. He left after a minor Indian uprising; perhaps you've heard of him?"

Hooper smiled. He was not yet thirty. He was a big-shouldered fellow with a weather-tanned face, and knew Jimmy O'Rourke had been long before his day. But there are names which are milestones in the history of the fur companies, and Jimmy O'Rourke's name was one of them.

"Now I remember," said Hooper. "I think everybody in company head-quarters knows that name – they told me he was something of a legend in these parts. People say he was fearless. Helped to put down that uprising you mention, mostly with tact and fairness, so I was told. It was the last we ever had in this territory, too. And you're his grandson? Well, I'm sure glad to see you at Bull Moose. Come and see me tomorrow; maybe we could go hunt a deer after I finish here. I'll show you the lie of the land."

The next day, when O'Rourke was again paying a visit to the trading post, an old Indian called Johnny One-Pine entered the establishment, bent double under the weight of his winter's trapping. He had two pack-mules outside too, both staggering under their burdens.

Many winters had left their mark upon Johnny. His hair was gray and greasy, and hung in wisps over a face whose skin was as taut as a drum; and his eyes were slightly milky, with wrinkled crows-feet at their corners. His frame was slightly overweight now. Yet Johnny One-Pine was still a chief of among the Kikiallus, and a mighty hunter, and even now was making a living from his trapping. He retained the respect of the younger braves as a man of wise counsels, and a fearless warrior.

He often reminded the members of his tribe that the land they walked upon was theirs and theirs alone, and though they should be wary of the white men, they should in no way, shape or form show deference to them. Nor suffer their land, or their goods, to be taken away by the whites. Furthermore, should a man or woman of their people be killed or injured by an outsider, white or otherwise, then he or she must be avenged. The length of time it took to accomplish this was irrelevant. 'A life for a life,' was the way of the Kikiallus people. Though many had forgotten the old laws of the tribe, Johnny had not. And from time to time he was wont not only to remind them of how things should be done, but to demonstrate the principal too – which led him into conflict.

Dumping his bundle of furs on the counter, a fine lynx-fur on the top, he nodded to Hooper and straightened up, his unclear eyes now resting on the other white man in a searching scrutiny.

And for a space of seconds, while Dan Hooper examined the top-most silver-russet pelt, there came back to those tired eyes flashes of the fire that had long been dormant. He stared hard at the eastern dandy in his over-smart clothes, and his gaze was not a kind one.

O'Rourke, seeing the gleam of those dark, piercing eyes, felt a sudden stab of nameless fear. His hands gripped tighter on the counter. He did not attempt to account for it, nor could he have explained it if he'd tried, but he knew he was suddenly in great danger. Johnny was an almost worn-out member of a dying race, while he was an educated white man from a city in the east. They were strangers with nothing in common. And yet – the Indian stared with a fierce hatred, as though motivated to attack at any second, filling O'Rourke with terror of the old man,

"Why's he looking at me like that, Hooper?" he stammered.

"Oh, he's just a little curious," said Hooper, unconcerned, busying himself with his scrutiny of the pelts, jotting down his findings on a scrap of paper.

There was certainly a terrible intensity in the old Indian's gaze. But why? They had never met before. James O'Rourke, although nervous of the native men, had a deep respect and sincere admiration for them. He was certain that his face had given nothing away that would offend the old chief, and yet, there it was, that unnerving hate-filled look.

After a minute or two, Hooper addressed old Johnny, and the Indian averted his eyes. Masking his hostility, he got on with his trading, unrolling his other packs and bargaining with the Company Man for the price of his harvest of furs. It was a lengthy business, for long experience had taught the Indian the value that white men placed upon his pelts, and each separate piece was the subject of fierce haggling.

And even when Johnny had received tokens in exchange for his furs, he showed no inclination to leave the post and return to the lodges of his brothers that were pitched a short distance away on the level ground in front of the timber-built cabin, the home of Daniel Hooper.

He flung his battered hat onto the counter and straightened his back. The others looked up, sensing that the old man had something important to say. When he saw that he had their attention, he begun:

"That man," he said, staring once more at O'Rourke, "would know why I look at him so, and so I shall tell you. Many moons have passed since I was young, white-men, and soon shall my time shall be over, and I make the long journey to another life. But listen, and I will tell you the tale of Johnny One-Pine, chief among chiefs."

He glanced around the room to make sure that he had the full attention of not only of the half-dozen Indians standing there, but also of the Company man, and his nervous guest.

"Long ago," he continued, "when many, many braves had lodges in my camp, I had a son, a fine and beautiful boy, and no father ever loved his offspring more than I loved him. He stood straight as an arrow and moved swift as an eagle. Dear to me as the light of the sun was he. He grew tall and strong – but never old. He should not have died. I would willingly have given my life to save his. Instead, after we fought side by side in battle, while he walks with the warriors of old, I am the one left here among the living, weighed down all these years with a heavy heart."

There was bitter, barely-concealed anger in his voice as he continued:

"It was foolish of us to think that we could drive the white-faces from the hunting grounds of our fathers. Yet my people had suffered many evil things, and so we led my people in the battle, and though he showed great courage he was slain."

For an instant Johnny's eyes rested again upon James O'Rourke, and they were milky and dull no longer; they shone again with a flashing hatred that the two white men had hitherto failed to fathom.

But even with his voice under control, his tone monotonous, but not his message, they began to realize the true depth of his feelings as he continued:

"In a forest not far from here, in our own camp, I was witness of his slaying. I saw the white-face who fired the bullet that laid my papoose in the grass, sent him too soon to hunt with our fathers."

The Indian fixed O'Rourke with another searing look, and held his gaze.

The youngster licked his lips. He could almost imagine that Johnny One-Pine was accusing him of having fired the fatal shot. Suddenly he wished he was back in his own city of the east, away from the raw edge of civilisation.

"He was an old man," went on the Indian, still staring at O'Rourke, "one of the men who, in those days, gave us beads and dull knives for our furs. My heart burned for vengeance, and for many moons through the winter and into the spring I sought my chance to slay him. But my chance did not come. In the springtime, the slayer of my son left the north lands, and never have I seen him since, though I sought him long and far."

He broke off suddenly, and turned to Hooper:

"See, now, the passing of many years on my face. I near

87

the end of my hunting. I would have a knife, White-Face. A sharp knife for skinning, and other things. That is my wish."

He thrust a few of the brass Company tokens into Hooper's hand. Some distance along the counter, James O'Rourke shivered unaccountably at the request, but Hooper appeared to see nothing odd in it. He knew that the spring trading was the occasion for the telling of many tales and much boasting; he had known Johnny during the three successive seasons he had been at Bull Moose, and the old man had never given him any hint of trouble.

So he pushed half a dozen long-bladed knives across to the Indian. Johnny One-Pine was long in making his choice, testing the edge of each upon the flat of his thumb, minutely scrutinizing the blades in a search for flaws in the steel. Finally he selected one that was long and supple and with the edge of a razor. It had a fine, sharp point at its very tip, good for many purposes.

"This one is good," he grunted; "Such a knife shall bring me to the end of my hunting. I was telling you all the name man who slew my own blood – his name was-"

And then Johnny paused. His flabby fingers closed up on the haft of the knife; he lifted it, his face appearing to regain in that moment some of his lost youth, and again he looked upon the young man from the wood-pulp company.

"His name," said the Indian, "was O'Rourke! And you are his blood. I see it plainly in your face."

In a sudden lightning movement he Indian threw his knife, and it stuck in the counter next to the young man's hand.

The man from the south gave out a high-pitched squeal of fear so strange, that it hardly seemed possible it came from the throat of a man. He cowered back, his hooked fingers clawing at the edge of the counter. Then, he half climbed, half fell, over the counter to Hooper's side to get further away from his assailant.

"Hold him back, Hooper, I think he's gone mad and he's going to kill me!" he shouted.

Nor was his ordeal yet complete. Swift and agile as a deer, the Indian sprang over the counter and landed next to O'Rourke. Never in his long life had the native man made a surer, more athletic leap than that one. The new knife back in his hand, uplifted, held trembling above the chest of the white man, the Indian's eyes flashed crazily with anger – but he did not strike. Hooper had grabbed the old man's arm, a two-handed grip of surprising strength that thwarted the Indian's attempt on O'Rourke's life.

For a second or two, the two of them stood locked there, swaying back and forth, the old chief's arm held shaking in that position, till suddenly he relaxed and he allowed Hooper to take the weapon from his grasp.

"Enough! Get out of here!" said Hooper, "Leave, and no more of that nonsense! This man had nothing to do with the things you speak of, so get it straight in your head."

As he spoke, he pushed the Indian backwards, guiding him through the opening in the counter and into the larger part of the room. From there he half-ushered, half-shoved Johnny One-Pine through the trading post door and out into the chill spring air. He threw the new knife out after him and closed the door.

The old man accepted all this more or less passively, but though it was the manager who put him out, it was O'Rourke he had glared at, bristling with hatred even as he was ejected. Hooper closed the solid door in his face and bolted it, then returned to his counter.

"We'll just leave that locked a minute," he said calmly to those in the store. "What a to-do, boys, I thought it was elephants that never forgot."

He shook his head sadly, before adding quietly:

"Still, I guess a man never forgets something like that, no matter how long ago it happened."

Then he turned to look at the quaking figure on his side of the counter.

"Hey, Jenkins," he shouted over his shoulder, "make us all some coffee, we've all had a bit of a shock out here. And bring that bottle of brandy from the cupboard – a little shot for medicinal purposes might be in order, I think."

A skinny wisp of a lad with ginger hair and freckles stuck his head through the back door, stared gormlessly at the occupants of the store for a moment, then disappeared once more to get the refreshments.

Soon O'Rourke was sipping his brandy-laced coffee, staring into space blankly. There were beads of sweat on his forehead, but with a great effort he managed to stop himself trembling.

The customers satisfied, and the door unlocked again, the two men found themselves alone with each other.

"He wanted to kill me," O'Rourke whispered hoarsely.

"The man's possessed. You've got to get him arrested and put under lock and key. He's going to knife me as soon as he gets the chance."

Hooper didn't deny that this might be the case; but he had a different view of things to the younger man.

"Maybe he'll try again," he nodded. "Johnny One-Pine belongs to the old stock. He's raw-red Indian under the surface, and he hasn't forgotten the blood chant and the war dances of his younger days, I can tell you that much. Yes – he may try something again, but it's up to you to see that he doesn't get the chance."

There was little sympathy in Hooper's voice. He was a man of the north-west, with the courage of his pioneer ancestors bred in him, and O'Rourke had shown about as much backbone as a worm. The truth was, the Company Man had no respect for those who handled themselves so timidly when the chips were down. He knew they had no place in that part of the world, where cowards were likely to be found out for what they were sooner rather than later.

"It might be better," he said, "if you were to quit Bull Moose altogether. Maybe Johnny'll forget you, maybe he won't. But the sheriff won't lock him up just in case he has another go at you. That Indian is the sort to stir up a rebellion to get what he wants – I've seen these things get out of hand before – and he can't be trusted. He's raw-red, as I said, and once he has a notion in his brain, there's no telling what he might do."

O'Rourke was horrified. He forgot that he was supposed to be scouring the district for promising tracts of pulpwood, and experienced a desperate home-sickness for the cities of the east.

"I'll go," he muttered, "I only just arrived and already somebody wants to kill me. Then you tell me nothing can be done. I never realized there was still no such thing as law and order in these parts."

"Well," said Hooper, "it isn't so much that there isn't law and order, it's just that folks have their own way of doing things around here. As for the Indians, the Company set itself up at Bull Moose Mountain to trade with them, so it's only right to try to understand them, and try not to get too upset when things go wrong. After all, we can't lock 'em all up. And, all things considered, it is still their land."

This was not the answer O'Rourke wanted to hear. He was packed and ready to go in a few hours.

But it was three days before he was able to leave the post. There was some difficulty finding a guide, for not a man from the crowded tepees near the store would undertake the duty. Hooper, who understood the local dialect, gathered that they would rather have guided a pariah. The old chief had evidently been busy, spreading word that the descendant of an Indian-killer was the man who might need their service.

And now One-Pine disappeared, silently as a ghost, vanished into the huge expanse of forest that surrounded the trading post and went on for dozens of miles in every direction. Several of the other native men had also upped sticks and left. Those left behind seemed less friendly, less willing to speak with Hooper. The white man regarded the signs as ominous, and saw James O'Rourke as an encumbrance. Though he had done nothing wrong, he had to go, and fast. Hooper was shocked to find out just how easily the trust and goodwill between himself and the Indians had been put into question. He redoubled his efforts to procure a guide, and found a man at last, a Canadian who went by the name of Pierre Lafitte, a rather dubious fellow, known for being a little too fond of whiskey. His one qualification for this job lay in his inordinate hatred of the Native Americans, an attitude that earned him the contempt of Hooper. But at least he was ignorant of the bad feeling welling up in the region. Otherwise, he too, would have refused the task of getting O'Rourke, the focus of the new hostility, as far away as

possible from the Kikiallus Indians.

The Company Man watched them go from the ancient, dilapidated stockade wall that enclosed the store, his cabin, and the cluster of tepees that made up the settlement. The Canadian was weighed down with the easterner's pack, while O'Rourke himself hugged his loaded rifle and looked about him nervously.

"They're going to run into trouble for sure," Hooper thought to himself, as they disappeared into the trees and were lost from his sight.

He was right. The very next morning, the Canadian came staggering back into the settlement, a bloody gash on his forehead and his clothes daubed with mud from the trail. He looked, and was, a man who had come near to the end of his resources.

Hooper let him into his office and snapped his questions at him.

"What on earth has happened?" he said. "Where's O'Rourke? Come on man, spit it out!"

The Canadian leaned back in his cheer, downing the entire cup of brandy he had been given in one go. Then he exhaled deeply and began:

"They've got him," he said; "I think maybe he's dead already - there were dozens of them, covered in war-paint, armed to the teeth, meaner than skunks, they were. And the big one, crazy as hell, he threatened to kill me too, unless I hot-footed it back here real quick. I thought he would do for me anyway with an arrow in the back, he looked that mad."

"What'd he look like, this chief?" said Hooper, though he already knew the answer.

"Ugly, big-boned fellow," said Lafitte, "pretty old too, with long gray hair and a real mean face. Got war-paint on all over. Looked like thunder. Kill you soon as look at you, I reckon!"

"That's Johnny One-Pine all right," said Hooper. "Sounds like half the tribe are with him. He's stirred them up on stories of past glories, and how bad they've been treated down the years, no doubt. Now they're up for anything and likely to get themselves hanged on account of it, the damned fools."

"Well maybe they should be hanged," said Lafitte, "A man's not safe round here no more. They got bows, tomahawks, war-clubs, and some of them got rifles too.

Jumped us soon as we made camp last night - we didn't have a chance. See what they did!"

He pointed to the gash across his forehead and spat venomously on the floor.

"First they clubbed me and left me for dead. Then that old one kicked me. When I moved, they stood me up again, pricked me with arrows and set me on my way back here. They took O'Rourke, and by the way they handled him, I'd say they're going to torture him a deal then kill him, maybe tonight."

"You mean he isn't dead already?" said Hooper. "How do you know?"

"They told him, in English, to scare and taunt him I'm sure, that he would be taken to the place where the chief's own son was killed, then die slowly there tomorrow. 'A life for a life,' that's what the old one said. He sounded crazy, but he'd got about two dozen men hanging on his every word, ready to do anything he says."     "I see," said Hooper coolly, scratching his chin. "Do you remember anything else they said?"

"Well, O'Rourke tried to tell them they would hang if they didn't let him go – which only made them all laugh. The chief said he would go to the hunting ground smiling because his son had been avenged."

Even before Lafitte had finished speaking, Hooper was on his feet, selecting items for his traveling pack. There was a grim determination in his eyes, a single-minded acceptance that he would have to put things right himself. Or perish in the attempt.

"They will only kill you too, Monsieur," said the Canadian, "surely you don't mean to go out there to meet them alone? I mean, what can you do? You are one man against so many."

"Where exactly was your camp?" said Hooper, checking his rifle; "How far had you got before they jumped you?"

"We had reached the end of the long straight valley where the woodland trail runs next the river. They went in the direction of Eagle Point, though it was a good few miles downstream. But monsieur, if you try to find them, you will be going to your grave for sure!"

"Eagle Point?" said Hooper, "I know the place. It's the last landing place before the rapids. They camp there from time to time – it's also the place where One-Pine's son was killed."

He quickly calculated the time the braves would take to get there and how long he might take to reach the same place – the spot where the tribe had met their last defeat, when Jimmy O'Rourke and a detachment of soldiers had fired on the mutineers all those years ago. Then he remembered with a start it could be more easily reached by water. The Indians would have several miles to walk to get there from the ambush site, but the Little Snake River that ran by the trading post led to within a few hundred yards of the old battlefield. Though there were rapids and some fast water to negotiate, it being the spring thaw season, the journey could be completed before dark.

Hooper nodded sagely to himself, and his mind was

made up already. It was up to him to rescue O'Rourke, and it had to be a single-handed job. The Canadian was obviously not up to the task, and he was in no condition to travel again that day. Jenkins, his young assistant, was not exactly an ideal companion with whom to face a tribe of warring Indians. Besides he was needed at the store to watch over the goods, some of which consisted of guns and ammunition, which would have to remain in storage just now, for obvious reasons.

Thus, Hooper would have to go alone. He was only moderately acquainted with the territory he would have to journey through, but he had a reasonable map which indicated the location of each flight of rapids, and an excellent birch-bark canoe to travel in. He knew the place he sought was to be found just past a wide and shallow bend. There, a sandy beach was overlooked by a great gray boulder reminiscent of a roosting eagle. This was 'Eagle Point', where O'Rourke the Elder had taken the soldiers so many years ago, to quell the Indians' unrest. Just inland was a grassy clearing, an ancient camp site, but latterly an area kept clear of vegetation only by the deer. There, the old chief's son had been killed, along with several other braves who dared to fight the soldiers. It was not a good place, given its history, and all things considered, to conduct a successful release of a prisoner of the name of O'Rourke. Hooper could only hope that his own good standing with the tribe would give him a hearing with old One-Pine, enough time to make the man see sense and let the young man go.

It was a risky business. Hooper's resolve to go down the

river to an uncertain fate was even more remarkable considering he did not even think O'Rourke a particularly valuable or worthy person to be saved. It was only that he felt partly to blame for the young man's predicament, and for the fact that some of his customers had decided to revert to warlike ways; and the Company had always taken the lead in keeping law and order in the region, the nearest sheriff being so far away as almost not to matter to those at the Trading Post. A certain sense of duty might have been Hooper's motive for going out to confront the tribe alone. But a sense of duty would not keep him safe if the Indians refused to heed his counsel.

Even as he packed up his gear, he thought it very doubtful that the braves would be talked out of their enterprise just because the man they traded with had come to scold them for breaking the white man's law. Nevertheless, he would not be able to live with himself, nor face his superiors if he did not try. That was the measure of the man the North-West Basin Commodities Company had installed to run their store at Bull Moose Mountain.

# CHAPTER THREE:
## A PADDLE TO EAGLE POINT

Barely an hour after his meeting with Lafitte, kneeling in a birch-bark canoe, Hooper embarked upon his lone quest. He had reckoned the length of his journey as ten or twelve miles, all of them by water. He had the current with him, though there were rapids to negotiate; but, barring accidents, he counted on making the landing before the ominously named Voyager's Grave Rapids by nightfall.

If his luck held there would be time enough then to rescue O'Rourke, for Johnny One-Pine, with an Indians love of ceremony, would most likely delay the execution of his vengeance until after the war-dance, the flickering lights of the camp fires, and a few bottles of firewater had spurred his warriors into a murderous frenzy.

He made good progress – better than any unexpected. The melting of the snows and had filled the river to the brim, and the current ran swift and smooth. By the early afternoon he had reached the shallow bends, after which he would find the stretch of sandy beach and the big rock of Eagle Point. He regarded this as enemy country, and placed his loaded Winchester ready to hand, while his keen eyes scanned the aspen thickets on either bank.

Somewhere ahead of him, he could hear the dull roar of the rapids, like the thunder of a far-off train, the greatest noise emanating from the steepest drop, in fact a sizable waterfall. Strictly speaking, the real 'Voyagers' Grave', where many a foolhardy traveler had met his end, was the churning, swirling pool below the fall.

Hooper felt the speed of his canoe, caught in the grip of the faster current, increase perceptibly, but he was not worried. He would easily be able to direct his craft over to the beach, his chosen destination, a hundred yards or more before the first of the rapids made things a little more tricky.

He knew that, had he needed to go further down the river, he would have been compelled to carry his canoe a good half-mile along the bank before being able to paddle again. The map was quite clear: 'Portage Here', it said. Shooting the rapids was virtually impossible even when the river was low. Now, while the river was swollen like this, the very thought of entering the rapids past Eagle Point made him shudder

With a tight lipped smile, Hooper dipped his paddle to bring his frail craft into the shallows, and almost at the same moment as he neared the bank he caught sight of the first painted face among the bushes. The young brave had diagonal stripes of war-paint on his face and bare arms. Another man stepped out of the undergrowth, clad in the tribal dress of brown buckskin trousers and shirt, with small, distinctive animal and bird shapes painted on in decoration. He had eagle feathers in his headband, a tomahawk in one hand, a war-bow in the other. On his back he carried a full quiver of white-feathered arrows. Other men similarly dressed and armed followed him. To Hooper, used to seeing most Indians unarmed and dressed in the cast-offs of the white man's wardrobe, the vision vouchsafed to him could mean only one thing: One-Pine's braves had been persuaded

100

to go on the warpath, and they were ready for a fight. They guarded the sandy beach where he wished to make his landing. They already looked fired up and ready to launch an attack.

A second later he received startling confirmation of the fact. The twang of a bowstring heralded the flight of an arrow which hummed viciously a few inches above his fur cap. One of the Indians rushed forward, hatchet at the ready, wading through the shallows toward him. Hooper reached for his rifle, aimed, but hesitated to shoot; he was reluctant to take the life of a fellow man. Besides, he would have no position from which to negotiate the prisoner's release if he killed a Kikiallus brave even before he landed. At that moment the fast water took him and he decided to paddle rather than fire.

Soon he was in the first of the rapids, but still able to get alongside the bank, which was low enough for him to grasp a willow branch and stop his canoe; but no sooner had he done so, than half a dozen Indians appeared out of the woods and ran straight for him. He pushed himself out again, and was immediately accelerated into the swift flow of water that was the hue of green bottle glass. The sound of rushing water was all around him as he fought to keep his canoe clear of the many knife-edged obstructions.

Once more he aimed for the edge of the river, but now the bank was solid rock and there was nothing to grasp, nor any sign of an eddy that might give him respite enough to haul himself clear. In any case, Indians were running along the bank, almost keeping pace with him as he paddled. They would surely fall upon him as soon as he attempted to scale the bank.

"Better the rapids than an arrow or knife," he laughed grimly to himself.

Jumbled impressions crowded in his brain, as he hurtled along in that glass-green, rushing water towards the point of no return, the lip of the highest fall. He could see a wall of mist ahead, masking the sheer drop into oblivion. He heard a mighty crash of waters falling bodily into space. Being a strong swimmer was unlikely to help: he knew that below big falls of water such as this the water churned and eddied so much that even a deer, a bear, a buffalo for that matter, would struggle to get out – never mind a man weighed down with sodden clothing and boots filled up with water.

For one instant his nerve failed him. With death ahead, and death beside him on the banks, as the taut bows bent and delivered their singing arrows, he stopped paddling, resigned to his fate. But then he sensed a slender chance, and almost without thinking, took it. There was a single tree with an expanse of branches dripping with moisture, hanging out over the last few yards before the fall. He dropped his paddle and adjusted his balance, then sat up on his knees as high as he could, his arms stretched upwards, as he struggled to keep his balance.

Already water was pouring into the seams of his canoe, the craft having been dashed against sharp rocks. With only a yard or two to go before the deadly drop, eyes glued to those over-hanging branches, he grasped the strongest bough within reach and clung on for dear life.

His judgement was good, and he found himself suspended; though the branch bent crazily, it did not break, leaving his legs in the water, but his upper body dry. He started to move, hand over fist for the rocky bank, and in a minute he was there, hauling himself onto dry land and panting with his exertions. Meanwhile, his canoe, with rifle, pack, and all his gear, had disappeared over the fall.

As he rose to his feet, a sharp kick sent him sprawling onto the earth again. Then there was a lance at his throat, held by one of the war-painted men of the tribe who were standing over him.

Hooper knew he would not live long if he tried to fight back. Save for the knife in his belt, he was unarmed. His rifle had gone with the canoe, sweeping down the rapids. He remembered with regret that he had unbuckled his revolver and put it in his pack to keep it dry.

Helpless, he faced a dozen Indians with painted faces and feathers in their head-bands in the manner of their ancestors. The men had tomahawks, war-bows, a lance or two, there were even a couple of old single-shot rifles. There was no sign of old Johnny One-Pine himself, for the moment.

Hooper knew that only a show of bravado would save him now.

"Greetings, my brothers," he said, rising from the ground, raising his hand in salute, "I have come to speak with Johnny One-Pine, your chief. You all know me. I am a representative of the Company and I seek a pow-wow. You know I mean you no harm. You must show me your camp."

The men did indeed recognize Hooper. Most of them had

a deep respect for him, and when Johnny One-Pine had persuaded them to join him and see the White-Face O'Rourke killed, they had not envisaged having to deal with the Trading Post representative. One of them, with a single eagle feather stuck in his long, black hair stepped forward:

"Follow me white man," he commanded tersely, adding, "It is not good, you should not have landed here."

"And you should not have tried to kill me," said Hooper boldly.

"If we had wanted to kill you," said the warrior, "you would already be dead."

One of the braves took Hooper's knife and shoved him forward along the path. A ten minute walk through the tall balsam thickets that fringed that part of the river brought them back to Eagle Point, beyond which was the clearing in which Johnny One-Pine and his followers had pitched their camp. There were about two dozen tepees thereabouts, with many warriors and their families going about their business, or gossiping among themselves. All stopped what they were doing and stared at the prisoner and his captors as they entered camp. Hooper was led to where the old Chief was sitting with some braves by a camp-fire. Women were roasting meat over hot stones ready for a feast. A short distance away was James O'Rourke, his hands and feet bound with cord, with a long rope tethering him to a tree like a sacrificial goat awaiting slaughter.

He looked at Hooper with sunken, tear-filled eyes, his expression one of terror. He opened his mouth to speak, but no words came out. There was blood on his clothes, and bruises on his face.

Hooper eyed the captive pitifully then turned to the old Chief, who indicated that he sit with him by the fire.

"Why have you come here, Hooper? If it is to plead for this man's life, you have wasted your time."

"I demand you release that prisoner immediately," said Hooper, staring him angrily in the eye, attempting to assert his authority on the situation.

The chief merely laughed, calling Hooper's bluff.

"You have no business here. This is Kikiallus land. Your laws have no meaning here."

"Let me take him back and I won't involve the sheriff," said Hooper. "Kill him and I'll see you all hanged."

"Not if you are dead too," said Johnny One-Pine coldly.

"I think you wouldn't do that," said Hooper boldly, "You have no quarrel with me – unless you harm that man. But remember this – I've always treated you and your tribe as my brothers. Many's the time I helped your people, tended your sick and gave food and shelter to the old. Traded with you all, fairly too. But if you think I am your enemy, go ahead. The sheriff and his men will hunt you down for it, mark my words."

The chief looked at him curiously for a minute, summing up the man who dared walk into his camp and make demands of him.

"No, Hooper. I shall not kill you. But you will return without this seed of O'Rourke. For many long years I have dreamed of this day, when my son should be avenged. You shall not stop me. When the sun goes down, by the cut of my knife, he shall die. It is right."

"It is *not* right," said Hooper, "that you kill a man who had nothing to do with your son's killing. This man would not take part in any fight against your people. Just look at him."

The chief gave a quick glance toward his weeping, trembling prisoner.

"He has the heart of a rabbit, it is true. But I will have my revenge. It is right."

"I tell you it is bad. If you kill an unarmed man like that," said Hooper aggressively, preparing to deliver his thunderbolt, "The Great Spirit himself will say you are a *coward!*"

The Indian snatched up his tomahawk and stood over Hooper, the weapon trembling in his hand for a second or two.

But then, his dark eyes flashing with anger, One-Pine lowered the hatchet and said:

"It is best you go now. I do not wish you dead, but if you call me coward again in front of my people, I will kill you, Hooper."

"Now look," said Hooper, in a quieter, more earnest tone, "You have shown this man and all your people you could easily kill him; isn't that enough for, that you have the power of life and death over him, that you could kill him if you wished? Why not show mercy, and remain free."

"I am already free, white man," said One-Pine, sitting down once more. "This is not the gift of your people."

"True, but it is also a fact that the white men from the town can hang you if you break the law. There is no place you can hide where the sheriff and his men cannot find you in the end."

"I care nothing for your sheriff and his soldiers-"

"Hear me out, Chief Johnny One-Pine. The law of the white man says that each of your braves that helped you could also hang. They'll be seen as accessories and be put in a noose the same as you!"

"No! I alone shall do the killing; I alone shall be the one to take a life for a life," said the Chief.

"Even so, the law is the law. But listen, haven't you and your men been christened by the old missionary that serves these parts. Didn't he teach you the importance of showing forgiveness and mercy to your fellow man?"

"All of us have received one of his washings in the river," sneered the old man. "But now we believe his medicine was false. We shall go, when we die, to our own place, not his. And this 'mercy' you talk of is but another word for *weakness.*"

"Nevertheless," said Hooper, deciding to change tack, "there is something you need to know. You have captured this man, who is only a grandson of James O'Rourke."

"He is the seed-"

"Hear me out. Yes, he is the seed, a grandson of James O'Rourke. But he himself has done nothing against you – or your son. The old man O'Rourke, he was a brave one, but see how this one quakes, see how unworthy he is in exchange for your brave son."

"If he is a coward, then all the more reason he must die," said One-Pine.

"No! Not so," said Hooper hotly. "If he is a coward, he is unworthy! I tell you, you plucked an innocent, frightened boy who just happens to be a grandson of the man you sought, to avenge the great warrior your son was."

"He is not innocent-"

"Yes, Johnny, he is!" said Hooper, pushing his luck, "And you're doing all this to heal an ancient wound that cannot be salved in this way. Do you think you will feel any better about your son tomorrow after this poor wretch is butchered? You're killing him for no good reason, and when you do, well, all these men will hang. Is that what you want?"

"They are sworn to me. All are prepared to die," said Johnny, avoiding eye contact now, staring into his camp fire.

"Die, yes, but for what? Will your son live again? Will any of these men be able to trade goods for their families again? What about their papooses, their wives? Think Johnny One-Pine, think like a chief. A wise chief too. I think you are a brave man. But to kill a man bound hand and foot like that. That would be like killing a helpless child!"

Once more the chief turned angrily on Hooper:

*"Enough!"* said One-Pine, "You chide me like a woman. You give me the twisted tongue of the missionary who told us everything we believed, every thought we ever had was wrong."

He angrily threw a big branch into the fire. Hooper could see the old fellow's brows were knotted in deep thought, which he believed was a good sign.

The two men sat silently staring into the fire for a good ten minutes before, finally, the old chief spoke.

"A life for a life, that is the way of our people. And of yours, Hooper: 'An eye for an eye, and a tooth for a tooth,' isn't that what your bible says?"

"Yes," said Hooper, "but it also says 'Vengeance is mine, I will repay, saith the Lord.' In other words, it is up to God, not man, to take revenge."

"Your God," said One-Pine, "not mine. And what will your God do if I break this law?"

"No happy hunting ground. Only a pit of fire," said Hooper.

"Words!" scoffed the Chief, "Foolish words, I do not believe them. What kind of god would not see the rightness of a life for a life? What kind of a god would deny a man his revenge? But listen, Hooper – I have changed my mind. But not because of you, white man. Your words are false."

"Sure they are Chief," said Hooper, guessing that One-Pine needed him to retract his words, so as not to lose face. "You'll let me take him away, then?"

He spoke this last phrase quietly, full of hope, until Johnny One-Pine released his own, final thunderbolt:

"No. He shall be given a knife and fight for his life like a man – or else die quaking on the earth, if he so wills it. That is my decision."

Before Hooper could react, the chief had conveyed this change of heart to his men, who whooped in celebration at the prospect of seeing the coward die in this entertaining manner.

"How?" said Hooper, over the noise, "How will you fight him?"

"Not I," said the Chief, "but my own grandson, Fishing Eagle. He will finish off the seed of Jimmy O'Rourke. Each shall have a knife and a tomahawk. The Great Spirit – or God – will decide who shall live and who shall die. And then you will know as we know, Hooper, that a life must be paid for a life!"

He rose and turned his back on Hooper. The interview was over, the course of action decided. Fishing Eagle would be the one to murder O'Rourke. Hooper's attempt at saving the easterner had failed.

By now the camp was in great commotion, more braves than before coming into the clearing, along with some women and children. From their midst, a young, muscular youth of about eighteen emerged, bare from the waist up, horizontal stripes of red and white across his face and body. He was unusually tall for an Indian youth, perhaps six feet, strong-armed and with big, bony hands. He had a long-handled hatchet in one, and a long, Bowie-type knife in the other. His expression was severe, but there was an unmistakable glint of pride in his eyes.

Hooper suppressed a groan of resignation. O'Rourke could not be saved now; yet still, he had to do what he could for the lad.

"Let me prepare O'Rourke," he said, "You must at least let me do that."

The old Chief nodded. A brave threw down at Hooper's feet an old tomahawk with a chipped, rusted blade, and a short skinning knife with its point broken off.

"You may cut him loose," said One-Pine, "and prepare

him for the fight."

Hooper took up the knife and tomahawk and strode across to O'Rourke. Freeing the prisoner from his cords, he spoke curtly and without pity.

"Now listen to me O'Rourke," he said, "and listen good. That kid over there by the fire is going to kill you in a few minutes unless you kill him first. You have to fight, O'Rourke, it's your only chance, d'you hear me?"

He picked up a skin of water and emptied some of it on the young man's face. O'Rourke, his hands and legs freed, rose unsteadily to his feet.

"But why, why do they have to kill me," he sobbed. "Tell them again they have to let me go. Tell them-"

Hooper slapped him hard on the side of his face.

"Quit that," he said, "You have a chance and you have to take it. Here, drink this."

He took from out his pocket a small hip-flask of brandy.

"Drink it," he hissed, "Now."

O'Rourke did as he was told. A little color came into his cheeks. His eyes seemed to focus, and he bent down and picked up his two inferior weapons. He held them firmly, weighed them in his hands, the tomahawk he took in his right, the knife in his left.

"That's the way," said Hooper, "Now watch his every move, he may be over-confident. If you get the chance, use the hatchet. Don't throw it, do a feint with the knife then strike. D'you hear me?"

O'Rourke nodded, his eyes narrowed in readiness, though his trembling lip gave away his fear. He stood up

111

straight, focused on the painted youth who stood motionless in the circle of warriors and squaws that had formed up. Without any further prompting, he stepped into the ring and took up a fighting stance, sideways on to his adversary, one foot forward, the knife in his left hand thrust outward, the tomahawk in his right hand held level with his shoulder.

"Good," thought Hooper, "At least he means to make a fight of it. I just hope he doesn't suffer too much when the end finally comes."

# CHAPTER FOUR:
## A FIGHT TO THE DEATH

With a shout from old Johnny One-Pine, the contest began. As the tribe whooped and screamed their encouragement, Fishing Eagle circled around his quarry, smiling craftily at the prospect of a swift victory. But when he finally struck out with his hatchet, a head-high swipe attempting a kill with one blow, O'Rourke deftly swayed back and countered with a tomahawk swing of his own, only missing his opponent's head by a whisker. The smile left the Indian boy's face; his grandfather shouted something by way of warning, perhaps that he take more care, that the bedraggled white man might not be quite the pushover they'd envisaged.

Hooper, more surprised than anybody, noted that O'Rourke had lost his mask of fear. His blood was up, and he was determined to do his utmost to survive. He began to use his feet to move about the ring on his toes, a skill, Hooper guessed, he had acquired when being schooled in boxing or fencing. When the Indian came at him again, making a feint-attack with his knife, and then sweeping low with his tomahawk at the white man's forward-most left leg, he was able to step back in time. But only just – he received his first injury, a harmless nick of his skin on his left knee-cap. The leg of his corduroy pants, slit at the knee, was soon crimson with blood. The din from the spectators grew louder, but Hooper saw that O'Rourke's stance was unaltered, and he breathed a sigh of relief.

Encouraged by having drawn first blood, Fishing Eagle

moved closer, sensing his victory; and when he landed a disabling blow on his opponent's right arm, and O'Rourke's rusty hatchet fell into the grass, the fight seemed practically over. Hooper groaned, as the boy from the city seemed to go into shock. He ceased to defend himself. His eyes were glazed and his expression vacant. His right arm was useless, and his left dropped harmlessly to his side. The young Indian turned to Johnny One-Pine, who motioned for the boy to finish it quickly by passing a finger over his throat. Fishing Eagle obligingly strode forward, went to the side of the helpless O'Rourke, took a very deliberate aim at the left side of his neck, and swung.

What happened next was so swift and terrible that even the blood-thirsty spectators were shocked into a stunned silence. As the Indian's tomahawk arced at O'Rourke's neck, the white man swayed back and thrust out his knife to parry the blade. The force of the Indian's stroke was so powerful, that O'Rourke's upturned knife blade passed clean through the two bones of his assailant's wrist. Screaming in pain, Fishing Eagle dropped both his weapons and fell to his knees, the knife still stuck there, the blood gushing out fulsomely from the severed arteries and veins.

In a second, O'Rourke had leapt on him, pushed him over and sat on his chest. Picking up the Indian's own shining knife from the grass, he pressed the blade to his opponent's throat, ready for the coup-de-grace. Hooper, the Chief, the braves, the women and even children, all watched mesmerised by the turn of events, and the imminent prospect of Fishing Eagle's brutal but necessary death. There was no cry for mercy – from any quarter.

But James O'Rourke never made that fatal cut. Instead, he withdrew the knife and cast it down, and stood up, staggering on unsteady feet.

Hooper was the first to react. The ultimate part of the fight having been played out just in front of him, he rose and caught O'Rourke in his arms, then set him down on the ground and yelled across at the Chief:

"A life for a life you said! Well, you got your life! Now give us ours!"

Without waiting for a reply, he went over to the stricken Indian youth and tugged the blade out of his wrist. From his pocket, as the Indians gathered round cackling confusedly like a flock of startled turkeys, he took out a handkerchief and tied it round the boys arm above the elbow, and tightened it enough to stem the flow of blood.

One or two of the warriors, still animated by the cruel excitement of the fight, drew their knives and made a move toward O'Rourke, but Johnny One-Pine stopped them in their tracks. He berated them angrily that they would kill a man who had, in effect, given Fishing Eagle a second chance. So far as he was concerned, the hostilities were over.

Thus, the victor of this most brutal of fights retained his life. He propped himself up against a tree, exhausted, injured, but alive.

This Hooper did not see, pre-occupied as he was attending to the Indian boy, who, though spared, was still in grave danger of bleeding to death. Though he knew the tourniquet would keep Fishing Eagle alive, he also knew that the wrist and hand would be lost if the flow of blood could not be restored. No physician himself, he did at least have an inkling of what to do, having assisted a doctor faced with a similar task some years ago. The fellow had saved the hand of a man when it had been almost severed by the bite of a grizzly. But would Hooper's inexpert attempt at surgery work here? There was nothing for it, but to take a chance.

By this time Johnny One-Pine and the boy's father, younger brother of the man killed by O'Rourke the Elder, had pushed through the throng and knelt down beside Hooper to see what he would do.

"Get me a needle and thread and a bottle of whiskey – firewater – and heat a knife in the fire till it's red," Hooper yelled, at no-one in particular.

The Chief relayed the order, and presently a woman brought him the whiskey. Fishing Eagle made little movement or sound, which made the task much easier, and even when the cheap whiskey was poured into his wound he barely flinched, evidently in shock after the blood-loss and intense pain. The wrist cleaned, Hooper could see the narrow blade had missed most of the larger blood vessels, which meant a better chance of
success.

"Hurry up with that knife," he shouted at the Chief and his son, "Red hot, mind you, and make it quick."

Within a few minutes a red-tipped knife was given him.

"You there!" said Hooper to the nearest Indians, "Hold him down, kneel on his shoulders. And get me clean cloth for bandages."

The knife hissed as it touched the broken blood vessels, and while Hooper cauterised them one by one, a foul smell filled the air. A little way into the procedure, the boy seemed to come to, and began to yell at the top of his lungs, only stopping after the skin had been inexpertly sewed back over the two gashes, and a makeshift bandage of shirt-cloth fastened tightly over it.

Only then did Hooper dare loosen the kerchief a fraction. There was a trickle of blood that stained a few spots on the bandage, but the crude surgery held up. Much to his surprise, the blood-flow was contained even with the band of cloth three-parts released. He explained to the Chief how the tourniquet should be loosened a little more each hour or so, but tightened if the blood flowed freely out of the wound. In time, the wound should heal, and Fishing Eagle keep the use of his hand. The old man nodded as if he understood, though Hooper doubted he had taken in much of his lesson. The fact that old One-Pine did not have the means of measuring the passage of an hour did not cross his mind until he was well on his way home – and he certainly did not lose sleep on the matter.

His duty completed, he rose and turned his attention to O'Rourke, who sat with his back against the same tree in the clearing he had previously been tied to. Hooper examined his right arm, which had received a fearful gash below the shoulder joint.

"Guess I was wrong about you," he said, preparing a bandage. "You've a wildcat in you after all."

"They still going to kill me?" said O'Rourke, holding one

hand over the wound in his arm, the other on the gash in his knee.

"Reckon not," said Hooper, as he began working on him, "But it's a long walk home on the river track. There's a trapper's cabin about five miles from here. We'll walk there, dark or not, before we rest – just in case they change their minds."

Before they left, the Chief, sullen-faced, came to watch Hooper tying the last of O'Rourke's bandages. He stood over them for a while, and Hooper sensed he had something to say; but eventually the old man turned away, without so much as a word, and disappeared into his tepee.

# CHAPTER FIVE:
## THE WEBLEY .455

That was the last time old Johnny One-Pine was seen by white men. A week later, the county sheriff and his men paid a visit to the camp site near Eagle Point, but found it deserted. Not a single person, Indian or otherwise, was to be seen there, or along the woodland trail to Bull Moose Mountain.

Then, while searching a lesser-known route through the hills, a mountain track used almost exclusively by the Indians, the sheriff found the shredded remains of a human skin tacked to a redwood tree.

"Is that what I think it is?" he asked his men.

He put the word out at Bull Moose, nearby settlements, and to anybody who would listen that there would be a thousand dollar reward for the person who gave the name of the victim, and that of the perpetrator or perpetrators. The informant would also be required to give evidence in court.

Needless to say, nobody came forward.

Nor was the victim identified, for old Sam Jordan had not told a soul that he was trapping in the area; and any kind of identification was impossible with only a fraction of the original human pelt left, thanks to the actions of bears, wolves, coyotes, crows, ravens and the like. The body itself had long been devoured by beasts and the scattered bones covered by the undergrowth.

At least it wasn't difficult to transport and bury Jordan's remains. How ironic that he should be rolled up and tied with some twine, before being dropped off at the undertaker's.

As for the old Chief, though certain of his braves ventured back to the Company Trading Post the following year, One-Pine made himself scarce, reputedly living out his final days with a few followers somewhere deep in the woods. One winter, the cold took him, and that was that.

James O'Rourke returned to his eastern city to recuperate, but a year later was back to source timber for his company, as he had been trained to do.

When Hooper saw him, he hardly recognized the young fellow. Full-bearded, upright, and carrying a bit more bulk, he was dressed more like a backwoodsman or trapper than a wood-pulp man. On one hip he carried a heavy .455 Webley revolver in a button-down holster; and on the other, a sheathed hunting knife, which he had the curious habit of touching on the haft from time to time as if to reassure himself it were still there. On his head was a well-worn beaver-fur cap, which he must have gotten second-hand. He was full of good-humored banter and bravado. Neither man felt the need to make reference to One-Pine or his men, nor of their ordeal in the forest, though as they conversed freely it remained the proverbial elephant in the room.

While the two men sipped the company's 'medicinal' brandy, poured liberally into cups of steaming coffee, the same celebratory drink they had partaken of after their return, alive, from the camp near Eagle Point twelve months back, Hooper noted that neither Indian nor white man were likely to give O'Rourke much trouble now. He seemed cocky, and self-assured; moreover, the Trading Post man received the distinct impression that the knife and pistol on his belt were not merely there for show.

The last Hooper heard of him, he was sourcing his pulp way up on the Canadian border. He had engaged a pair of Indian youths – not Kikiallus, but Flathead – to carry his gear and scout for him.

And he did have reason to use the Webley .455, and the hunting knife, as it turned out. The problem was a charging moose, and not a man on the war-path.

The story goes, he disturbed a big bull during the rut, the two came face to face, and a little altercation ensued. While the Indians made themselves scarce, there was a bit of shouting and bellowing, some branches and earth torn up and even a shot fired in the air.

Then the beast attacked; and it was the moose who came off worse.

THE END

# BOOK FOUR...

# THE PRAIRIE THIEF

*'Starting out ahead of the team and my men  folks, when I thought I had gone beyond hearing distance, I would throw myself down... and give way like a child to sobs and tears, wishing myself back home with my friends.'*
Young woman pioneer, 1860

# THE PRAIRIE THIEF

## CHAPTER ONE:
## THE STOWAWAY

**The big prairie wagon, the first of the fifty or more that made up the train, negotiated the ford with ease despite the depth of the water.**

But, after gaining the far bank, the marshy strip beyond the river engulfed its wheels to the axles and the team of a dozen oxen proved incapable of moving the lumbering vehicle, despite the vicious cracking of the teamster's long whip about their ears.

Trader Snowdon, captain of the caravan, rode up and briefly surveyed the situation, then gave the order, that the wagon be unloaded and the goods carried to dry ground, leaving the oxen only the empty cart to pull.

Ruben Martyn heard the command, and knew that at last his discovery was inevitable. Resolved to face mutters boldly, he crept from the nook where he had ridden in the wagon for the last week, ever since the train had set out from Fort Davey on its long journey across the plain. He dropped to the ground at the end of the wagon just as the first men began the task of unloading. He stood there unabashed, a tall, striking lad of seventeen, in his buckskins and brown leather hat, dressed for the plains, but the product of a Virginia farm where he had lived until the disturbances of the war changed his life forever.

His father, having sold up and headed west, had bade Rubin, his only offspring, to wait back east at a relative's house. But Ruben had grown desperate for the news of his pa that never came. So now, he too was heading west, with only the vaguest of ideas of how he would eventually find his father. Hiding among the commodities, emerging only at night, he had survived a week living that curious lifestyle, traveling ever westward; but now he was discovered, and braced himself for the inevitable dressing-down and, more importantly, the consequences that were sure to follow.

"Man alive, where on earth did you spring from?" a leathery-faced old waggoner gasped. "Hey, Sailor, it looks like the pair o' us bin carryin' a passenger all unbeknown!"

The man addressed was a jolly-looking giant, who had evidently abandoned the sea for the lure of digging gold; for these were the days when the Californian and other gold fields were drawing folks from all over the world. The giant grinned down at Ruben.

"Hey now, mates," be roared, "I've heard ye call these wagons of yours prairie schooners, but I'll he keelhauled if I reckoned on finding a stowaway aboard one of 'em. That's it, me boys – we'll call him the Prairie Stowaway!"

The laughter that went up was interrupted by Jeff 'Trader' Snowdon pressing his horse into the group. Ruben gazed up into his stern face fearlessly. He had approached Snowdon at Fort Davey begging to be allowed to travel with the train, and had offered either to pay or work his way. The trader, however, had considered his party already too large to handle without difficulty, and pestering by any number of would-be fortune hunters over the years had made him unsympathetic to Ruben's attempt to tell his story. Because his slender funds would not let him wait until the next caravan was ready to start for the far west, Ruben had taken the desperate course of stowing away in one of the wagons the night before the train set out.

"Who are you, boy, and what are you doing here?" Snowdon demanded; but before Ruben could reply, the trader had recognized him. "Wait. Ain't you the young kid who wanted to join up with the train back in Fort Davey? I remember your spinning some yarn about wanting to get to the diggings in search of your father."

"It was the truth I told you," Ruben Martyn retorted hotly, "and I offered to pay you what I had, but you wouldn't take it."

Snowdon's firm mouth relaxed to a smile.

"And what exactly would I do with *five dollars*," he laughed.

"An' I said I'd work my passage too," yelled Ruben, stamping his foot as he lost his temper at being made such a fool of.

"All right boy, don't get so riled," said the Trader more quietly, "Guess if you've got this far without my permission we can't turn you loose for the Indians to scalp. Work your passage, eh? So what exactly can you do, sonny?"

"Well," said Ruben, "for a start I can fight. I heard there's Utes in these parts'll scalp a man as soon as look at him."

"Uh-huh," said Snowdon, "You heard that about right. You got a gun, boy? Otherwise, how're you proposin' to kill them Utes."

"I got me a bayonet," said Ruben foolishly, as the men, hands on hips, roared with laughter at him. But they had a shock coming.

"Laugh all you like," he said, unsheathing a long army-issue bayonet he kept on his belt, "I ain't scared of no Indians. Killed me four Yankees with it in the war, big an' ugly as you fellers, too."

That wiped the smile off their faces all right.

Snowdon, who'd himself ridden with Jeb Stewart's cavalry two years before, but kept his mouth shut about it these days, looked the boy over again, saw him in a different light now.

"None of that sort of talk here, kid," growled Snowdon. "Folks are tryin' to forget. Put that toothpick away, and help those men unload that wagon before I change my mind."

Thankful at receiving such lenient treatment, Ruben set to work with a will. It was a long job getting each of the wagons emptied, and the contents carried piecemeal to the rise beyond the soft ground. It was also a struggle against time. Snowdon insisted that the last wagon must be over before night, for he knew the Ute Indians, who were indeed masters of this area, were on the warpath, led by their great fighting chief, Yellow-Hand. And it would be disastrous for their attack to find the white men's force divided into two by the river.

By the time that the last wagon was over and the big vehicles drawn into a tight, defensive circle, Ruben was almost too tired to eat his supper; but his labors had won him some encouraging words from Snowdon.

Next morning, when breakfast was barely finished, Snowdon summoned everyone to gather near him by a loud blast on his whistle. Ruben went with the others, and saw the train captain standing by a wagon which he recognized as the one that he himself had ridden in. Snowdon's expression was grim and angry, and Ruben felt vaguely uneasy while waiting for him to begin speaking.

"Men," cried Snowdon harshly, "something has happened in this here outfit we've got to try to clear up – and right now. I guess most of us are surprised to find we have a thief amongst us, but I've had an ugly proof of his presence."

He paused, and an angry murmur ran through the crowd.

"It'll be a lynchin' job if we catch the skunk, cap'n!" a man shouted, evoking a chorus of approval.

"You mostly know," continued Snowdon "that I'm takin' a big supply of goods across to my stores that are scattered up and down among the diggings. Waal, also I was carryin' a large sum of money with me in notes and coin for the diggers, who often come to my stores to turn their nuggets or dust into real currency. That money I carried in a hiding-place built into the rear axle-trace of this here wagon – a cache which I thought was known only to myself and the smith at Fort Davey, who fashioned it to my instructions. But seemingly I was mistaken. When I examined the wagon this evening to see if yesterday's strain had done any damage, I found the cache had been broken open and the money gone."

129

By the time that Snowdon had finished speaking, Ruben's brain was awhirl with recollections of something which had occurred one night while the caravan had slept. He had awakened to hear movements beneath the wagon in which he lay, and the sound of subdued voices. One voice had risen above the others – a whining, high-pitched voice that had something disturbing about it. Using vile language, and threatening horrible violence, in hushed tones a leader had addressed his men. He had urged them to keep their nerve and do as they were told, in no uncertain terms. Apart from his violent manner, there was something else that that distinguished it from the others, too: this man stuttered in an uncommon manner. As to his message, Ruben had overheard a phrase here and there, as the stuttering man talked, urging his companions to keep their voices down and 'get the money and hide it where no-one will look.' Then had come the muffled sound of splintering wood below him.

Only half awake at the time, Ruben had given little thought to the matter, either then or since. It had been none of his business, and he had hardly been in a position to investigate. Now, however, it all came back with a rush, and he was shocked to learn the full implications of the incident. He was about to move forward, to tell Snowdon his experience, when a big hand gripped his shoulder, and he was thrust before the crowd until he found himself face to face with the train captain.

"Say, boss," growled Ruben's captor, Kentucky Joe, "weren't that the wagon this young whipper-snapper were stealin' a ride in? Mebbe he's wise as to where the dollars hev gone to."

Ruben angrily wrenched himself free and drove his fist into Kentucky's leering face.

"Anyone that calls me a thief is a stinkin' liar!" he yelled at the company, then turned to take another swing at Kentucky Joe. It took two large men to restrain him till he cooled down a little. Only then was he able to gush out what he had heard to Snowdon.

Indignation made him tangle his story in the telling, however, and the fact that he had been prompted into speaking had prejudiced Snowdon against him. Reading the cold suspicion in the Trader's eye, Ruben began to stumble worse and worse until he came to a lame conclusion that sounded, in layman's terms, plain stupid.

"I guess it's no good asking if you could pick out any of those men you speak of," commented Snowdon sarcastically. "It would have been too dark to see them, eh?"

"I could identity one o' them," replied Ruben. "I should know him by his voice, even if I had to pick him out of a million folks."

The boy's unexpected assurance surprised Snowdon; partially convinced that his story was true, he decided to give Ruben a chance.

"If that's the case, sonny," he said, "you shall hear every man in this train speak, and if you spot your man, just tell me."

A method of test occurred to Ruben, a tongue-twisting sentence with which kids at his school had always been tormented. Here was a trap certain to catch a man afflicted

with stammering, even if he could otherwise disguise his voice. It was an unusual method with which to trap a thief, but at Snowdon's bidding, man after man
was asked to come to the front and repeat the sentence.

Most of the men stumbled over the words, some angry at the performance, some grinning; but one after another they took their turns – without the stammering man appearing.

"I guess that's the lot, boy," announced Snowdon at last, and into his tone doubt and annoyance had crept again.

Crestfallen, Ruben let his eyes wander over the crowd that was watching him with grim amusement. His gaze fixed upon a man who stood well back, held by the gleam of enmity with which the face was regarding him. Ruben's memory for faces was a good one, and he was sure this man had not come up for the test.

"We haven't heard everyone yet," he protested. "What about that man over there."

All eyes followed Ruben's pointing finger – then the boy was surprised to hear a great shout of laughter go up. He looked at Snowdon for an explanation.

"You've sure set me a puzzle there, boy," smiled the trader, "if you expect me to make a *dumb man* speak."

"It's more than me an' my pards here ever managed, cap'n," put in Kentucky Joe, "an' we've knowed him fer a pile o' years!"

Snowdon dismissed his men, before he turned to a shame-faced Ruben, who believed he had made himself look even more ridiculous in his efforts to prove his innocence.

"Now, boy," said Snowdon, just describe to me that voice which you expected to hear."

Ruben did so, Snowdon watching him keenly all the while.

"Ever heard of a man named Stammering Sam Blundell?" the trader asked crisply.

Ruben shook his head.

"Waal," continued Snowdon, "Sam Blundell is an outlaw, one of the worst criminals in the territory, and there is a big price on his head. I've never crossed his trail, but I believe your description of that voice would fit him exactly. Say, if your tale is true, and if Stammering Sam Blundell was in the camp that night, we need to know where he is now. We've put the entire outfit to your test without finding him. It's got me stumped."

"Couldn't the thieves have followed the train, and crept in to do the job?" suggested Ruben.

"It's possible," admitted Snowdon, "but it's also mighty improbable. Every night the corral is surrounded by a ring of sentries, most of 'em trained Indian fighters, and I'd back them to let nothing bigger than a mouse get past. I guess we can't do much in the matter now, but there's a sheriff at Kenzie Rock, the first settlement we touch on the other side of the plains, and maybe he'll handle the case satisfactorily."

He curtly sent Ruben to his work, and the boy went, hanging his head and feeling that suspicion still hung heavily over him.

133

## CHAPTER TWO:
## INDIAN ATTACK

The Utes had planned their ambush well, and their attack came with the suddenness of a thunderbolt. The caravan was crawling along in its usual double line, traversing a valley through some low hills, when there came the report of rifles, and the scouts, who had been riding out on the left flank, came galloping back over the skyline.

Hard at their heels rode a body of warriors on lean, fast ponies, their whooping growing ever louder as they approached the unprepared emigrant train below them.

Snowdon's shrill whistle signaled all to form a corral, and the twin lines of wagons divided, while the long whips of the teamsters cracked in emulation of the rifles, which were already hurling lead at the Indians.

The lines of wagons should open out and then the leaders close in again, so as to form a closely locked circle of vehicles from behind which the men could hold off many times their own number of Indians. But Ruben saw that it was going to be a terribly close run race to complete the ring before the Utes reached them. Let the Indians once get among the wagons, and all would be confusion. The white men would be caught in scattered groups, and their superior numbers would give the native men their victory – which would involve a wholesale
slaughter of every man, woman and child in the train.

Ruben had been served with a rifle and ammunition, and his allotted place in case of an attack was with Sailor, to defend the first wagon of the right-hand column. The two of them ran alongside the vehicle as it thundered over the boulder-strewn hillside, and, as the lines began rapidly to converge, arrows from the advancing Indians streaked through the air.

The gap grew narrower and narrower, and it looked as if the white men must just win the race. Then, the redskins concentrated their aim at the leading teams of oxen. Half a dozen animals went down, mortally wounded, and their companions piled on top of them. With a clear space of some twenty yards yawning in the wheeled stockade, the Utes screeched their triumph, and flogged their mustangs in anticipation of speedily getting in among the wagons.

Ruben had seen the danger as soon as the oxen had fallen, and he ran on at his hardest. Alone now, he stood in the gap as the first brave swerved his horse to enter.

For a second he squinted along the barrel of his Springfield at the painted face, and it seemed that no sooner had he pulled the trigger than the man pitched to the ground. The rider-less steed reared in a frenzy of terror, and as it wheeled about it drove two other mounted Utes into a collision, dismounting both. Sailor came panting up to Ruben's side, and blazed away with his Colt Dragoon, the six shots completing the temporary demoralization of the Indians, causing them to draw off.

"This is only a lull between the squalls," grunted Sailor as he reloaded. "There's old Yaller-Hand, musterin' up his boardin' party afresh, blast his eyes! They'll be on us agin in a minute – so be ready, boy, load fast and shoot straight!"

Ruben tried to fit his bayonet on the rifle – to no avail, for it was designed to fit a Richmond, not a Springfield, and merely dropped off.

"Damn stupid Yankee rifles!" he cursed, and stuck the bayonet in the ground by his foot in case it were needed.

Back came the Utes again, this time with their great war-chief himself in the van. But the delay, brief though it had been, had enabled Snowdon and a dozen others to join the two in the breach.

As the Utes swept on, Ruben fired once, reloaded and fired again; now the horses were almost on top of him. With the barrel of his empty rifle, he guarded a stroke from a tomahawk, but the shoulder of another mustang sent him sprawling on the turf. Hoofs thudded about him, missing him by mere inches; then he scrambled up again, finding and brandishing his long knife – the Confederate sword-bayonet he had used during the war – in place of the rifle he had lost. Eighteen inches of tempered steel, kept oiled and sharp, it was a formidable weapon in itself, as the Indians soon found out, and much to their cost.

The thin line of white men filled the gap, holding the main body of Indians back. But Yellow-Hand had already won through to the inside of the ring with a score of braves and was now turning to take the line in the rear. The plainsmen defending the wagons were sparing as many men as possible to keep up a covering fire on the breach, but they could do little about the enemy inside their circle for fear of hitting their own comrades.

Beset from front and rear, Snowdon and his companions

fought desperately. Yellow-Hand rode down on Snowdon, who was fighting back to back with Ruben. The Trader fired the last chamber of his revolver at the chief, but his aim was hasty and it was the horse that he struck. Fatally shot, the horse made a convulsive spring and came down on top of Snowdon. Jumping clear and rolling over to lessen the impact with the ground, Yellow-Hand leapt to his feet and advanced to finish off his helpless foe with his tomahawk in one hand, a knife in the other. But Ruben saw what was about to happen, and sprang to bar his way.

The chief's hatchet blow missed, but a lightning knife thrust nearly ended Ruben there and then. He narrowly escaped his death by a sideways contortion, though as it was, his shirt was ripped across by a foot or more, causing him to drop his bayonet. The stroke had, however, overbalanced the native man, who almost fell, and in a second, Ruben was grappling with him. He managed to pull the tomahawk out of the chief's hand and without thinking swung at him. That short-armed stroke proved to be a fatal blow to his opponent's skull, sending Yellow-Hand downward onto the grassy plain. From the way he fell, it was clear to all he was not going to get up again. Another brave, with more aggression than method, rushed straight at Ruben – a big mistake, as instinct and experience kicked in:

"*Yaah-hooooo-ah!*" yelled Ruben Martyn, crazy-eyed and fearless, thus treating all and sundry to the blood-curdling notes of a rebel yell, as he swung his tomahawk and lunged with his bayonet, "*Yaah-hooooo-ah!*"

A second later and the Indian was down; nor did not he

long survive the terrible wounds to his chest and throat.

Now Ruben positioned himself defiantly over Snowdon's body, awaiting more close attacks; but two other braves who had seen Yellow-Hand's fate dropped their weapons and a strange sequence of events now unfolded. The Indians stooped down, gathered up their chief's body, ignoring the flying bullets and hullaballoo of war, and bore off their senior's corpse, that it could be properly mourned and dealt with according to Ute lore. They fled on foot back out of the gap between the wagons, bearing the chief's body between them by. The death-song of the Utes was already on the men's lips as they ran, alerting their comrades to the fate of the chief.

The white men let the corpse-bearer and his companion go. What followed was almost magical: every Indian took up the dirge, and, chanting mournfully, they turned their backs on the white men, gathered their wounded and headed for the open plain. A few last shots by the wagon train men and women sent them on their way.

"I guess we've seen the last of 'em for a while," said Snowdon, once Ruben and Sailor had released him. "Yellow-Hand always claimed to be invulnerable in battle, but you, sonny, have shown them all his medicine was false. That will confuse them a good while, I'll be bound. And I have you to thank for my life, and the whole outfit too, for you likely saved all of us when you killed their chief. Say, boy, you fight like a cornered tiger!"

Ruben, covered in blood, looked down at the ground, abashed, as he shook the Trader's hand amid the thronging plainsmen.

"Lucky we had you with us, stowaway," said the Sailor.

"Well fought, son," said Ben Rogers, the Trader's second-in-command, gripping his hand in gratitude, "You sure gave them Utes a taste of their own medicine!"

Others came up and shook his hand – though not Kentucky Joe, or the half-dozen or so in his team.

The praise was still foremost in Ruben's thoughts when Snowdon sent for him that evening. The train captain was sitting alone by a camp fire and he beckoned the youngster to him.

"You'd better tell me all about that father of yours you've been seeking," he said.

Ruben's story was a simple one. His mother had died when he was small; the war had left his family penniless and destitute. While both father and son had fought with Lee's Army in the latter stages of the conflict, they had returned to find their farm razed to the ground. His father then set out for the gold fields in Montana, while Ruben lodged with an uncle's family. A few months after that, a letter had been sent there informing Ruben that his father had found a wagon master, and was duly setting out for the far west. But that had been the last his son had heard from him; for eighteen months or so he had received no news. Ruben simply had to try to find him – or learn news of the fate that had befallen him.

"I guess you've set yourself a big task, sonny," said Snowdon thoughtfully, when Ruben had delivered his tale. "I'm sorry son, but you need to be ready for disappointment or maybe bad news. What with the perils of the plains, and the evil sort of men found on the mining settlements, it's easy for a man to come to grief, or end up sick and trying to survive. Then, too, the west is a vast place to hunt over. Say, if you only had a photograph we could pass it around among my boys to see if any of them recognized him. Can't promise anything though; the chances are pretty slim."

Ruben did indeed have a likeness taken just before his father had left home. He handed it to the Trader.

"Hey, Palmer, Rogers, Barnet," he shouted to his head men, "Any of you seen this feller before somewhere? Up at Kenzie Rock mebbe?"

Palmer glanced at the photograph and shook his head; Barnet studied it more closely, before passing it on. Ben Rogers started as he looked at it, held it closer to the fire, then looked at Ruben with sadness in his eyes. It was a while before he spoke.

"I'm sorry son," he said softly, "If this man's your pa, I'm afraid you've come too late. This man's at peace with the Lord now; he's died son, further up the trail, at Kenzie Rock."

"No!" said Ruben, swaying on his feet, then clinging to the side of a wagon as the impact of Rogers' words hit him. "That can't be! My pa's alive, you hear me? He's alive, an' waitin' for me up ahead!"

Hot tears of desperation stung his eyes, and he struggled to compose himself before the sympathetic faces of the men.

"No, son, if your pa was Ben Martyn from Virginia," said Rogers, "I'm afraid he's at peace with the Lord now."

"But how?" wept Ruben, "What could've happened to

140

him, Mr Rogers? Surely you must be mistaken!"

Rogers cleared his throat uneasily, glanced at the Trader for support then continued in hushed, respectful tones.

"Your pa – Ben Martyn – he was the sheriff's man, used to keep jail and help out when folks get rowdy."

"My pa's Ben Martyn all right," Ruben managed to say, "but he said he was headin' for the gold diggings in Montana. I've been waitin' on news of him nigh on two years. Said he would write back soon's he could."

"Can't explain why he didn't write," said Rogers, but this is what I do know – he was on Bill Simmons train, eighteen or more months back. Everyone at Kenzie Rock knows his story. The feller met with an accident pullin' a woman clear from a runaway team, got a busted leg that laid him low for a long time. They had to leave him there in Kenzie – he had more of a chance of gettin' himself right again in town. When he was up and about again, around on crutches, he'd lost his pack and goods somewhere, an' they didn't have much luck finding them. With his leg in a state like that, he took to helping out the sheriff, an' from what folks say, he was a brave man. He was lame, but he kept jail, an' backed up his boss when the chips were down; and that's how he came to... pass away."

Ruben had slumped onto the prairie grass, sitting with his back against a wagon wheel, his face buried in his hands. After a minute or two he looked up, and forced himself to say:

"Please go on, Mr Rogers, I'd be mighty obliged if you'd tell me what you know."

And again he composed himself, holding back the tears and wiping his face with the back of his sleeve.

Two men helped him to his feet. Another handed him a tin cup with a good swig or two of whiskey in it.

"Drink it," ordered Snowdon, "Then we'll hear the rest of the account. Only, finish that first. You've had a shock, an' it'll help some."

Ruben managed only a few sips, almost choking on the strong liquor, his mouth and throat burning, his head beginning to spin.

Presently, Rogers continued.

"I hear'd it happened six months back. A gang of six armed men wearin' masks rode in, held up the town's bank. The sheriff and Ben Martyn were gunned down when they tried to stop them. They didn't stand a chance. If it's any consolation, Marshal Tom Blackamore's posse caught up with the gang two weeks later and all bar one of them varmints was killed."

"That's right," said another plainsman, "I hear'd the marshal run them boys to ground on the way to the border an' roll'd them boys up in a blanket, yes sir."

"But you say one got away?" said Ruben.

"So's I was told," said the plainsman, "but if ol' Tom Blackamore couldn't catch him, then nobody could – the man's got a nose like a bird-dog, so they say. Feller was an army scout, too, 'fore the war."

Jeff Snowdon laid a hand lightly on Ruben's shoulder.

"I'm truly sorry, son – I'll try and arrange you a passage back east soon as I can."

"No need, Mr Snowdon," said Ruben, "I've no intention of ever going back. That news won't stop me goin west. I'll go

142

pay my respects to Pa in Kenzie Rock, then find this Blackamore feller. Then it's Montana or California for me. But Sir – Mr Snowdon..."

He paused and looked down shamefacedly at his boots.

"Shoot son," said Trader Snowdon, "Anything I can do, jus' let me know."

"Just this," said Ruben: "I'd like to stay with you, till I cleared my name of the suspicion of you and your men. If my father had ever hear'd of me bein' accused as a thief, why he'd have killed me with his bare hands."

"Jumping snakes, boy," said the Trader, "you were clear of any of that the day you and I stood side by side fightin' those Injuns. I never heard tell of a crooked sort fightin' the way you did. Forget it son, there's my hand on it."

They parted for their berths soon after, the men with gloomy faces that the youngster had been given such dreadful news. As for Ruben, he managed to place his bedroll under a wagon and pull a blanket over himself; but he lay there awake most of the night, shaking with bitter emotion as he tried to come to terms with his loss. Only in the early hours of the morning did exhaustion at last allow him some fitful sleep.

The next few days were painful enough, but things were made all the harder to endure by Kentucky Joe and his crew, who took pains to remind him, either with their dirty looks, or by turning their backs on him, that a cloud hung over him still. And they were not the only ones to give him the cold shoulder. His heroics in the fight now forgotten or disregarded, few, except the Sailor, gave him so much as a courteous word to acknowledge he was there.

Gradually, he found strength within himself to bear his crosses manfully. But though his grief eased just a little, his burning shame at being treated by some as though he were indeed the prairie thief gnawed at his soul, and he longed for a way to redeem himself.

# CHAPTER THREE:
# GUNFIRE

Almost a month later, Ruben was tending a fire which acted as a beacon to the slower teams coming in to camp. Their final task was the crossing of a ford in the darkness. It had been late when the caravan had arrived at the river, but Snowdon had been keen for all to cross it before camp was made. By reaching the western bank they would avoid the train being hindered by the rising water level, as it had been raining heavily all day. And though the Utes had been defeated some way back, there was still an outside chance of an attack by way of retaliation.

With the prospect of reaching Kenzie Rock before dark the next day, Ruben was feeling full of apprehension and sorrow. Tomorrow, all being well, he would finally get to pay his respects at his father's grave. Only a few hours earlier a party of buffalo hunters had reported that Marshal Tom Blackamore was staying in a hotel in Kenzie, being in town to lend support to the latest county sheriff, who was, like most men of his calling, struggling to maintain some semblance of law and order in the territory. Ruben meant to meet this marshal, and find out what he could about the circumstances of his father's murder.

Remembering that the theft of the Trader's money would be reported to the sheriff of Kenzie Rock when they arrived, Ruben was keen to allay all suspicion over him before he arrived – though that did not seem likely as things stood. He consoled himself with the thought that, whatever might be

145

said of him by others, his father would never know his son had been suspected of stealing from another person. Though innocent, he still burned with the shame, made all the worse by the fact that he had never, nor would ever, steal – even if his very life depended on it. That was the way the boy had been brought up. Ironically, though he had been ordered to kill his fellow man in battle, not even a bloody war or the hardships it brought in its wake could induce him to break the eighth commandment and take another man's goods. War, he considered was war; but honesty was a matter of personal honour and a measure of self-worth. But how was he to prove his innocence to the doubters, once and for all?

He was brought out of himself by Snowdon shouting to a teamster who was just getting his wagon clear of the river bank.

"All across yet?" he said.

"All of us bar Kentucky Joe's outfit," the other man answered, "and the darn fools seem to be settin' up camp over there."

"Wonder if somethin's wrong with them," muttered the Trader. "I told them earlier they needed to cross this evening. If them fools get stranded tomorrow, it's gonna hold up the whole train."

"Shall I slip across to see?" offered Ruben, and at Snowdon's nod ran down the river bank and waded into the river. The long prairie trail had made him used to worse things than a wetting.

On emerging on the other side he made for a fire that gleamed some way back from the river. The light got brighter

146

as he grew closer, and it was then that he heard voices raised in an argument. Suddenly he was brought to a standstill, for one voice had risen higher than the others, bidding them all be silent – and Ruben had recognized that stuttering malevolent way of speaking instantly.

The voice had only uttered a few words when it was drowned by a bellow from Kentucky Joe.

"Who's that skulkin' about out thar? Com into the light, pard, an' let's hear yer bizness!"

Hearing the click of a hammer being cocked, and realizing that he had been seen, Ruben hid his feelings as best he could and advanced into the light. While he stated his reason for coming, he felt the half-dozen men seated there were watching him suspiciously, but with affected carelessness he glanced round them. In addition to Kentucky Joe there was Dummy and four others – and all of them had successfully passed the test by which Ruben had sought to identify the stammering thief.

But the thought which came to Ruben made his heart race. He knew now that the Stammering Man was close by. If not one of them, he must be hiding in the shadows. Ruben tried to maintain a straight face, to look unconcerned; but it wasn't easy.

"You can tell the cap'n we couldn't get the team to face the water, kid," said Kentucky Joe. "It's mules we drive, not oxen, and the pesky things cut up awkward. We'll be over as soon as daylight comes, high water won't stop us."

Ruben nodded innocently and turned away. He knew the man was lying. So, halfway across the ford he let himself be carried away in the current, drifting downstream a hundred yards, then swam to the bank he had just left. He was anxious to confirm his suspicions before he alerted the Trader.

Having snaked his way back to a spot from where he could just make out the low tones of the camp-side conversation, Ruben was rewarded by witnessing an apparent miracle. Dummy had discovered the gift of speech!

"N-Now s-see here," he whined, "I'm b-boss of this h-here outfit, an I'm gonna have my say after pl-playing dumb for so l-long," he said. "Any ob-j-jections?" He was fingering his gun and waving it about in the air as he spoke.

"Lookee here," said Kentucky Joe, "Nobody's trying to cross yer, Sam, surely you know's us all better'n that."

The name by which he was addressed sufficed to convince Ruben. Dummy was indeed the notorious Sam Blundell. Breathlessly, he continued to listen while the outlaw detailed his plans. Fearing a sheriff's enquiry into the robbery, the gang had stopped on this bank with the intention of turning south on horseback with the stolen money. The only thing stopping them now was that their horses needed some rest and to feed a while, after the day's exertions, having been ridden or tied on leads behind the wagon. Furthermore, the best time to slip away would be in the early hours while the other members of the train were asleep.

Ruben was just beginning to wriggle his way backwards, preparatory to giving warning to Trader Snowdon, when a pair of knees drove into the middle of his back, depriving him of air. Two big hands closed on his throat.

Before Ruben could regain his breath sufficiently to

struggle, he found himself bound and gagged.

"P-put him in the w-wagon," stammered Sam, "an get r-ready to saddle up an' light out before they c-come cross the river lookin' fer the k-kid. We'll drop him in the r-river later, afore we g-go."

Two men stooped to pick Ruben up, but their fingers never touched him.

"Hands up the lot o' you!" said a commanding voice out of the darkness. "Sharp's the word, if you know what's good for you, and don't even think of touchin' those guns – I got the whole lot of you covered, and remember this – the reward is for dead or alive and I'm not fussy – so watch yourselves!"

As the six pairs of hands went into the air, a tall figure in a long sheepskin coat came out of the shadows by the river. His whiskery face was partly obscured by a wide-brimmed black hat, and he was preceded by a pair of menacing Colts with extravagantly long barrels.

The sight of him seemed to galvanize the Stammering Man into desperation. He leapt sideways to shelter behind Kentucky's big frame, drawing his gun as he did so. Kentucky, guessing what came next, dropped to the ground, exposing Sam once more, just as the shadowy man pulled his triggers.

Before Blundell could fire, he fell to the ground with a pair of bullets to the heart, and a score of men rushed forwards to secure the others without a fight.

"Don't shoot! The money's in the flour-barrel," said Kentucky Joe windily, picking himself up. As they tied his hands behind his back, he added: "We ain't done no killin, Sir – that was all Sam's doin'."

"Waal, now, thanks for that," said the lawman sarcastically, "though it won't help you none – as accessories to murder, y'all gonna swing anyhow!"

Meanwhile, Snowdon cut Ruben's ropes.

"Easy, sonny," he said, as he released him, "You've done good, real good. Thanks to you, we bagged these varmints before they cut loose. I'd suspected they were the real thieves all along, though I couldn't prove it, so I sent for the Marshal. This is Tom Blackamore, come from Kenzie to meet us."

"Howdy son," said Blackamore, holstering one gun and shaking the boy's hand. "You the one that crack'd ol' Yeller-Hand on the noggin' with his own hatchet?"

Ruben only winced as his hand was crushed in that of the law-man.

"He's the one all right," said Snowdon, answering for him, "An' thanks to him we got Blundell and the whole gang. Judge Thompson's gonna be mighty pleased to see 'em sittin' in his courtroom in Kenzie Rock. Ain't that so, Marshal?"

"Mighty pleased," said Blackamore, "Scum like them allus slips up sooner or later. Took a boy to ketch 'em out this time."

"What'll happen to 'em now?" said Ruben, finding his tongue at last.

The marshal fixed him with his fierce, hawk-like eyes.

"We hangs murderers and thieves in these-here parts, sonny," he said; "There's a mighty handy tree outside town does the job jus' fine."

He laughed quietly to himself at the thought of this, then laid a hand lightly on Ruben's shoulder.

150

"Ben Martyn's boy, ain't you?" he said.

Ruben nodded in assent, the look on his face showing the marshal he'd already been given the bad news.

"He was a good 'un," said Blackamore, "standin' up for his boss like that."

He cleared his throat uncomfortably, then continued.

"Anyhow," he said, "we shot all them bastards bar one; feller named Hutton, went way down south. Reckn's he's safe; but he reckn'd wrong. Feller's got a thousand on his head now, an' I aim to collect. Fancy a bit of a ride through some hot sand, sonny?"

"Me?" said Ruben wide-eyed, "Why me?"

"Waal, now," said Blackamore, scratching his chin, "let's see. The Trader says you chopped down a chief with his own hatchet, along o' several of his best braves, then single-handedly tracked down Stammerin' Sam and his gang. Plus I hear'd you wiped out half the Union Army with a goddamn bayonet! I'd say that qualifies you somewhat to assist a U.S. Marshal in the course of his lawful duties – wouldn't you?"

"I guess," said Ruben, still not believing his luck.

"The pay's fifty cents a day plus food an' ammunition. Now – can you ride, boy? I mean *really* ride."

"You bet," said Ruben.

"Fast as a Comanche with his ass on fire?" drawled Blackamore.

"Pretty much, Marshal," said Ruben.

"Then get yourself one o' them gunbelts," said Blackamore, "pick a nag an' foller me. First we runs these sons of bitches over to jail, then off we hops to Mexico, by the dawn's early light."

The marshal paused, as if something was bothering him.

"Oh yeah," he said, "Find yourself a big canteen an' a fancy hat, son, 'cos where we's ridin' it's hot enough to melt your goddamn nuts off."

"But what about sleep, Marshal?" said Ruben, gathering up a canteen and stifling a yawn, "I've been up since an hour 'fore dawn. An' then there's them Utes."

"Sleep?" said Blackamore drily, "You kiddin' me, son? We either sleeps when we gets to Kenzie or when we's dead, whichever comes sooner. As for them Injuns – with you an' that knife walkin' round in the dark, I'd say them's the ones needs to worry."

The talking done, they set to work.


The Trader and his men helped prepare a strange-looking caravan for its journey. In a short time the marshal led a string of five prisoners down to the river, each one tied on a mule. Next came Ruben on a big gray horse, a pack-pony trailing behind with Blundell's body slung over its back.

One by one the horses and mules entered the swirling water, and plodded gamely across. Snowdon, Rogers and the other plainsmen stood and watched them go, until the rearmost shape, a dead man wrapped in canvas on his last rough ride, disappeared into the shadows of the far bank, on his long, dark trek into town.

## THE END

# BOOK FIVE...

# HANGING FEVER

*'Hang 'em first, try 'em later.'*
Judge Roy Bean

# Hanging Fever

## CHAPTER ONE:
## A DANGEROUS TRIP INTO TOWN

**It was all quite simple. The Salt Hill boys were going to put one of the Long Fork outfit in a noose and hang him till he was dead.**

Nor were they much fussed which one they lynched. That's the nature of a Prairie Vendetta: someone's got to die. Someone's got to pay. Sometimes it's for a good reason. Sometimes not.

Either way, someone from the enemy camp gets it, usually when he's not expecting it, and not quite ready to die.

Alex Sanderson was not quite ready to die.

And he had no idea of the danger he was in, as he casually rode into town whistling happily to himself. Thinking of that little drink he aimed to have after running his errand had put him in a good mood. Sent into Four Springs to pay off some money his boss owed at the Saw Mill, he was about half way down Main Street when a black-toothed old man that was chewing tobacco on the shady side of the way, just outside Golightly's General Store, called out to him:

"Hey, you! One of the Long Fork outfit, ain't yer?"

"What's that to you?" said Alex, pulling up for a moment.

The old man stepped out into the sunshine and, looking

up and down the street to make sure they couldn't be overheard, then said in a confidential low tone:

"It's lucky I see yer, son. You don't wanna go no further this mornin', no sir. You see them bunch o'horses tied up outside Van Allen's saloon?"

Alex looked down the street, and sure enough, there were a bunch of horses outside the Golden Star saloon.

"What of it, old man? Is it a raffle? I don't mind a dollar ticket, if that's their game."

"Raffle nothin'," said the old timer, "Don't ye be fresh young feller. There's a dozen o' the boys from the Salt Hill Ranch in the bar, and they've bin' laying out for one of yer this month past. Reck'n they're gonna string someone from Long Fork up, no questions asked, so take a turn and tote the other way out o' town, if yer knows what's good fer yer."

"Thanks," said Alex, "but I take my orders from Old Man MacAdams, an' so long as I draws my pay from him, not the likes of them, I aim to go to the saw-mills. 'Sides who are they *really* laying out for? Not me, I bet. I've had no truck with any of that crew."

"Hah! Any of yer's good enough fer them," said the old chap, "One's as easy to hang as another, fur as they's concerned. Ever since you boys headed Tim Lyall off your place and into the arms o' the law, they've sworn it's gonna be a neck fer a neck, an' they mean to ketch one of you boys and swing him from the same tree as the sheriff hanged Tim Lyall."

Alex knew the name. Lyall had been one of the Salt Hill crowd, till he quit his job there and took to horse stealing.

There was a story going around too, that Lyall had killed a girl in another state and was wanted there. One day, he turned up at the Long Fork Ranch, but Old Man MacAdams refused him a job owing to his shady reputation. So Lyall was sent away. It was later discovered he'd been riding a stolen horse, and soon after that the sheriff arrested him while he was drinking with his old pals and locked him up. The Salt Hill outfit believed that MacAdams should have given him the job, and a chance to straighten out, but the truth was nothing could have saved him once he took the path to horse-theft. The fact that the boys from the Long Fork bunk-house had told Lyall what they thought of him was neither here nor there. Nor was it true that anyone from Long Fork had tipped off the sheriff about Lyall's misdemeanors or his whereabouts; but the Salt Hill boys nevertheless got it into their heads that his capture and hanging was pretty much their fault.

"Surely," said Alex to the old timer, "they won't start a fight in your respectable little town with the sheriff just across the way?"

"No," he said, "but there's fifteen miles of open country 'twixt you an' yer bunk-house, young feller, an' they'll be after yer like greased lightnin' once they see yer try fer home. They're a rough lot at Salt Hill and they've sworn a vendetta agin your lot."

"Well, all that's mighty interestin' "said Alex, "but I've got to go on down the town anyway. Thanks all the same for the warning. I'll keep my eye on 'em."

Alex rode past Van Allen's without anyone coming out to look at him, and did what he had to do at the sawmill, then set off back down the main street.

This time he was seen. There was a bunch of fellows outside the saloon engaging in horseplay, but they stopped and stood staring in stony silence at Alex as he passed. One of them gave a wink, and he knew he'd been recognized, and that trouble was sure to come to him now. He thought of the long fifteen miles between himself and home, and there was a sick feeling in the pit of his stomach. It was doubtful his nag would be up to much in the way of galloping all the way back, having already walked the fifteen miles into the town. So what was he to do now?

Alex thought for a minute, then lit down off his horse and hitched him to the rail and went into the bar, followed by the Salt Hill crowd.

He got himself a drink. The Salt Hill boys said nothing, but there were knowing looks passed between them as they eyed him over. There were seven of them in the bar room, more of them barring the way out, and he thought of how he might get all of them inside where he could see them.

As they continued to give him the evil-eye, Alex leaned across to Van Allen and said loudly: "Surely you don't intend to allow shootin' in here, do you?"

"Not 'less I does it myself," said Van Allen, glancing at his shotgun leaning up on his side of the bar. "Why?"

"Oh, nuthin'," said Alex, "Glad to know I can take my drink peacefully without gettin' plugged."

"You bein' funny, young feller?" growled Van Allen as he swabbed down his counter.

"Not so much funny," said Alex, "as jus' a little nervy to

be stared at by a load of Tim Lyall's friends – with their hands nearly touchin' their irons. Ain't no call for that sort of thing today."

"I'd shut it, if I were you," said a big fellow with a sombrero, his eyes glaring at Alex, black as thunder. A few more of them gave tongue, bringing in the ones from the doorway to see what was going on.

"Waal, you're mighty brave," said Alex, "when you're twelve agin' one. But I'm finishing this here drink, see, an' if any of you want to start somethin', just remember Mr Van Allen's got a gun with a hair trigger for unruly customers like you."

That did it. They gathered round him like dogs round a grizzly, yapping and gesticulating but never quite coming in for the kill, while Van Allen laid a hand on the barrels of his gun. Alex knew that if he left now, his chances of not being followed and getting home were about nil.

"Heard about these boys and their great vendetta, Mr Van Allen?" taunted Alex, "Seems they aim to hang me to get even for Tim Lyall. The way I see it, their quarrel's with the sheriff, not me."

"What you talkin' about?" said Van Allen. "Hain't heard nothin' bout no vendetta."

"Waal, you soon will," said Alex. "Now I ain't gonna start shootin' in your house 'cos your rules don't allow it, but I'm gonna start shootin' as soon's I get outside. It's twelve to one, so I'm within my rights."

"What!" roared Van Allen, picking up his gun and waving it around, "I'll have no gunplay in my saloon! Git outa here

159

young feller and don't come back."

He leapt the bar like an athlete and lurched towards Alex to show he meant business. The fortunate part of all this was that the Salt Hill boys had taken their hands away from their pistols and were gaping at Van Allen to see what he would do next.

Alex finished his drink and looked about him, wondering if he had bitten off a little more than he could chew. Then he remembered his plan and streaked for the door before the big bar owner reached him. He was outside, had his horse unhitched and was up in his saddle in a matter of seconds.

"Hey boys," shouted Alex, "I'm out for trouble and I'll shoot the first one of you comes out here! And the second one, too, you bunch of cowardly coyotes! Twelve to one, is it? Come on over to Long Fork and see what you get!"

But never a one spilled out onto the street. Instead, it was Van Allen who came out and stopped up the doorway with his big body, the barrels of his scatter-gun swinging this way and that. Though he was a man with many faults, Van Allen, was no coward, putting himself between the two factions to stop them shooting at one another.

"You outside, now git!" he yelled, "An' you inside stay put. He's a crazy 'un! He's pi'son! Let the crazy feller take himself off, an' none o' yer move!"

Luckily, the Salt Hill lot didn't want to show their hand too plainly right there, where everybody could see. So, despite their rage, they did as Van Allen told them, and Alex managed to get away with none following.

Alex grumbled back at Van Allen a bit at first; but when

he got to the end of the street he was off like lightning, till he knew nobody was going to catch him. And so he got back to the ranch with the message that the Salt Hill outfit had got a halter waiting for one of them.

# CHAPTER TWO:
## A NECKTIE PARTY FOR BILLY

Much to his surprise, the boys didn't take too much account of what was threatened.

"They talk a lot of hot air, them fellers," said Pete Hanlon, the foreman, when Alex told his news in more detail that night at supper. "It won't amount to nothin'. This is a law-abidin' country, and if the sheriff will hang a man for horse stealing, it stands to reason he'd do the same for murder, and they know it."

So, they didn't think there was too much to worry about. After all, prairie vendettas were a thing of the past, of the time when free grazers, ranchers and farmers were in bitter disputes over boundaries and suchlike. To tell the truth, there were other concerns that overshadowed the matter, namely that a terrible dry spell had been going on for weeks, and all the livestock was under threat. The steers would stray for miles and miles in search of water, so that the men had to ride out to turn them before they wandered out into the great sandy plains, where there was no chance of moisture, and where they would have perished miserably.

The Long Fork boys found themselves up in the saddle for up to sixteen hours at a stretch, day after day, heading back stray bunches of cattle to decent pasture within the boundary, where a sufficient supply of water was to be had.

Alex put the thought of a vendetta to the back of his mind and got on with the tasks in hand. One morning he was

162

out with Billy Wymark, a good pal of his, tracking some beasts as far as the boundary line when they lost the trail. They were casting around for it when Billy suddenly called out:

"Jee-roo-salem!" he hollered.

"Found somethin' Billy?" asked Alex.

"Sure," he said, "but I don't know what to make of it. Lookee thar!"

He pointed, and Alex saw there was someone riding towards them. He looked to be an oldish man with a long white beard, spectacles and a black coat and hat. He was riding a gray horse and carried a big book. When he got close, he lifted a hand and said:

"Young men, greetings!"

"Howdy!" said Billy.

"The cattle stray from the pastures," said the old man, "and so does man."

"Meaning us?" said Billy, amused.

"Meaning the folks of the town of Four Springs," said the old man. "I'm a missionary, and I'm on my way to convert 'em."

"Bully for you," said Billy, "They sure do need it, and then some. But did you see a bunch of strays on the way across? We're missing a few hereabouts."

"I sure have," said the man, "if that is what you seek. There – just behind that hill, my boy. He pointed to a sort of mound called Juan Hill that stood by itself on the otherwise flattish plain, not half a mile away.

"If you'll take an old man's counsel," he said, "you will

separate and go one to the right and one to the left, passing round the hill on opposite sides, and so you'll get the beasts between you. If you both go chasing round on the same side you'll only scatter them further off, I reckon."

"Sure," said Alex, "That makes horse sense."

"So long mister," said Billy, "You rub it into them folks at Four Springs good and hard."

"And give a good big rub to old Van Allen in his saloon," said Alex, "he was using language fit to make your hair curl last time I was there!"

He started off towards Four Springs, to do what he could for Van Allen, or so the ranch-hands mused. Billy and Alex rode together for a spell, then headed for opposite sides of the hill, so as to get the steers nicely between them ready to drive them back to the better feed on the ranch.

The two men were feeling glad they'd fallen in with the old bible puncher, for it looked as if he'd saved them some trouble. They expected to see the beasts just over the hill, cropping on the scanty herbage thereabouts. But then, coming round his side of the rise, Alex saw something that stopped him dead in his tracks. Not cattle, but horses. And on every horse, a man, and on every man's face bar one was a mask! The only face unmasked was Billy's, for reasons plain to see.

"Glory-be!" thought Alex, "Now I see their game!"

He had twigged that the old man with a beard must have been one of the Salt Hill crowd, wearing his disguise and going to a deal of trouble to separate the two friends. With his lying yarn of lost cattle, he'd lured Billy into a trap set just behind that hill. Their game was to make off with Billy and carry out their revenge on him as pay-back for the hanging of Tim Lyall. Evidently, they meant to carry out their prairie vendetta, crazy as it seemed to Alex.

The whole posse rode off just as he sighted them; and he was so mad, he let out a whoop, drew his gun, and pelted after them. At first he gained on them, and he loosed off at their rear-most man, who was all in black like an undertaker – or a preacher. For then he saw that it was the man that had tricked them so easily. He would have given a year's pay to have dropped that man. But the distance was just too great. He was almost out of range. And there was also his friend Billy being galloped off in the midst of them to think of. There was a chance of accidentally hitting him with a bullet meant for the others, so he put away his gun.

The old timer in town had been right – the mob were taking Billy to be strung up, over at Oak Tree Ridge, where the only decent trees to rise up out of Sage-Bush Prairie were to be found. That was where the sheriff had hanged Tim Lyall. It was a good ten miles away, as a bird would fly. But there was no straight route to it. There were two ways of reaching it from Juan Hill – the right-hand one which would bring the riders within three miles of the homestead of the ranch, or the left-hand way which was a deal longer, and would oblige them to bear off round a rocky bluff, and cover some rough ground where the going would be slower. And that gave Alex a notion. It was just a chance. He couldn't follow the whole lot of them and fight alone. But if he drove his nag all out the way, and streaked for home, there was a chance he might pick up some of the boys, and they might yet be at Oak Tree Ridge before the others came up with their prisoner.

Billy's life was at stake. He turned right-handed, though he didn't like losing sight of them; and put his head down and rode for home at such a lick it felt as if the wind would blow his hair clean off. He had never ridden like that before; and he hoped he would never have to again. He knew all the while that a stumble would settle Billy's fate, and that he carried his one poor chance in his hand.

## CHAPTER THREE:
## THREE BOXES OF SHELLS APIECE


When he got to the big house, he saw Old Man MacAdam talking to Pete Hanlon. He tumbled off his nag and hollered out:

"They've got Billy and they're gonna hang him up at Oak Tree Ridge!"

"Who's *they*?" roared the old man, going purple in the face.

"The Salt Hill bunch. They gone loco. But we might be in time if we leave now!"

MacAdam and Hanlon glanced at each other for a half-second, but the news sank in almost at once.

"They're not right in the head!" said the boss. "Oak Tree Ridge, you say? Well, let's sort it boys."

Then Pete and MacAdam got busy and inside three minutes had found three of the boys, and saddled a fresh horse for Alex, making up a group of five in all. There was Pete Hanlon, Three-Fingered Jake, John Smith the Britisher, and Jimmy Burns. The old man came out of the house carrying an armful of Winchesters and a bag of ammunition. He tossed them a gun, and three boxes of shells apiece.

"You'll need these," he said, "I'd go with you if I carried less weight. Riddle them skunks, if you have too. They started it: now go and finish it boys!"

They said no more, but set out for Sage-Bush Prairie, eight miles away.

They passed their boundary mark five miles out; and then there came a bit of rising ground. With that in front, they couldn't see the plain yet. And when they got to the top of the slope, they scarcely dared to look down, till John Smith gave a sudden cheer.

"It's all right, Alex," he called back, "There's the old tree and there's nothin' on it yet!"

Pete was leading them straight towards the tree. There was a water hole a little short of it, and the water in it was very low now, so that they could walk with dry feet over most of it, and find cover deep enough so that men and horses were out of view – and shot – from the plain.

They got down into the hollow and dismounted.

"Let 'em come close," said Pete, "and then we'll let them have it. Keep down boys, the nags won't leave the water, they'll be all right." He grinned as he squinted down his rifle.

It seemed as if they'd never come.

Alex felt he'd been waiting there hours and hours, when at last a horseman came riding out of the end of a gulch, way over to their right. And then the whole bunch of them followed. Alex couldn't see Billy at first because they were so close around him; then they opened out, and it was easy to pick out Billy, him being the only one not wearing a mask.

They came on, trotting easily. The plain was a rough place, all scrub and rock and prickly cactus, so that none wanted to cross it carelessly. They reckoned, no doubt, that they weren't pressed for time. But they'd reckoned wrongly.

They were four hundred yards away; then three hundred; then two, and still Pete kept flapping his hand, low and out of their enemy's sight, to make his men hold their fire and stay put. He'd reckoned that one sudden volley might end the business, make the masked men turn tail and run.

But things don't always happen the way they're meant to. One of the horses down at the water took a fright at something, scrambling up out of the pond, and then galloping off. Heads went up on the enemy side, they were warned now. Ping! went a rifle from their side and the horse stumbled over.

At that moment Alex and his comrades upped and fired. They scattered then, the Salt Hill boys, and tumbled from their horses, taking cover among the rocks. There was only one man left mounted, and that was Billy. He couldn't get down: they'd tied his legs under his horse.

They were mighty spry, the Salt Hill lot, crawling and shooting without showing much of themselves, till it looked as if they'd soon have Alex and his pals surrounded. Shots came whistling in from three sides. Presently there was a yelp of pain and Jimmy went down.

Then the fellow that got Burns began to home in on Alex, but nobody dared loose off so much as a snap at him. The reason was that this man was standing behind Billy's horse, using him as cover and guessing, rightly, that no one the other side would risk shooting close to the very man they'd come to rescue. He'd just lean out from his cover and fire, then hide himself again. Nor could Billy kick his horse and get away, for he had a noose of rope round his neck which the rifleman behind him held.

Alex stood it for it a while, wincing as the bullets

ricocheted off the rocks around him, then resolved to get that tricky customer or get plugged in the attempt of it. Seeing Jim fall was the final straw. Scrambling out onto the level, he snaked his way from boulder to boulder, flat on the dusty ground.

At first he thought some of the Salt Hill bunch had seen him, as bullet after bullet sang close around him; so he flattened himself behind a hillock and lay doggo for a spell. Then he crawled a few more yards, and lay still again. For perhaps a hundred and fifty yards he crawled like this, till he got to the side of Billy's horse at about a seventy yards distance.

He saw the fellow crouching under the horse's legs, loading his gun. Then he peered round the horse and raised himself ready to shoot. It was a high-stakes game he was playing; and, not surprisingly, he lost. For at that moment Alex fired, and got him.

"Go, Billy, go!" he yelled, and Billy kicked his nag so hard, and screeched so loudly, that it lurched forwards and made straight for the pond with the rope still trailing from his neck. Luck was with him, that the cord didn't snag on a bush or rock, or that would have done for no-hands-Billy, bolting to safety among his friends. As it was, Alex watched the horse and rider gallop right over the lip of the pond and disappear in a cloud of dust.

Five minutes later Alex was there among the men. Billy had survived: in fact he had taken Jimmy's rifle and was alternately loosing off rounds and cursing his kidnappers.

It seemed the enemy had all they wanted for the time

being, for they drew back, some of them carrying wounded men. Alex, Pete and the boys laid off them as they did so, letting the Salt Hill bunch mount up and ride for home. The rescuers were glad to see the last of them, being almost out of shells.

Meanwhile, Billy put down his rifle and came to shake the hands of each of his friends in turn, Alex last of all, saying:

"You're one up on me, Alex, you sure did save my skin. I kept hearin' that feller say he'd put one in my back if I so much as raised a foot, so I was mighty relieved to see that one go down with a slug in his shoulder. Saw another one hoppin' on one leg, so that's two down for one of ours."

"Saw a third one bein' carried off none too healthy," said Jake. "Shot him plumb in the ass as he tried to crawl back."

Jimmy Burns had some paid leave, being nursed in the big house at Long Fork, fussed over by the boss's tender-hearted young daughter. Then, when he was almost better, his wound got infected and two days later he died. So the Salt Hill lot had their victim after all.

Old man MacAdams was apoplectic. He sent word into town that one of his boys had died at the hands of a Salt Hill mob for no good reason at all, and he wanted something done about it. Otherwise he'd see to it personally that the sheriff, the mayor and God-knows-who would lose their jobs. Either that, or he'd take his boys over to Salt Hill and shoot or hang the lot of them.

The talk amongst the boys in the Long Fork bunk house was all about who the sheriff would arrest, lock up and hang for the abduction of young Billy and the killing of Jimmy

171

Burns. But it was another month before the sheriff finally rode over to hear their side of the story. He tried to dismiss the near-hanging of Billy as 'a bit o' horseplay', and the shooting of Jimmy as 'self-defense in a fair fight.'

MacAdams threw him off his land.

Then the sheriff went over to the Salt Hill bunk house, asked a lot of questions and took down a lot of names. Finally, he went back to his office and slept.

"If you're still waiting for those rogues to be charged, boys," said Old Man MacAdam in the yard one day, "don't hold your breath. Sheriff's taking the easy way out, same as ever. In our part of the country, you got to protect your own and make your own justice."

Turns out he was right. No charges ever came. Nor were there more reprisals from either side, despite some savage talk. The unwritten rules of a Prairie Vendetta – unlike a family versus family feud that might go on for years – were that each side took a chunk out the other and left it at that.

THE END

# BOOK SIX...

# THE MAN FROM FORT DEFIANCE

*'Cowards never lasted long enough*
*to  become real cowboys.'*
Charles Goodnight.

# THE MAN
# FROM FORT DEFIANCE

## CHAPTER ONE:
## A MAN PREPARED TO FIGHT

**There was an air of deep gloom hanging over the tiny Arizona town of Holbrook the morning Skinny Rivers rode in.**

Rivers noticed something peculiar in the attitude of the cowboys and ranchers lounging along the town's main street, but he thought little of it. At the moment his one concern was rest and refreshment for his hard-ridden horse and himself. The last four hours of his ride, begun before dawn, had been under a brassy sun across the arid, cactus-dotted landscape. Yellow dust, mingling with the perspiration, had caked uncomfortably on horse and rider, and Rivers' throat was parched. His mount, too, hung its head, padding wearily along, coming gratefully to a halt when Rivers checked it outside Holbrook's only saloon.

He slipped to the ground, tossed the bridle over a nearby post and pushed open the batwing doors. The prickly heat had penetrated even to the saloon bar, but there was a smile on the face of Sam Sturridge, the saloon keeper. It was the only smile in the entire town at that moment, and Sam himself felt that it was as out of place as a joke at a sheriff's funeral. His full, round, brick-red face, however, fell into the natural folds of a smile, and it was only by great effort that he ever succeeded in looking serious.

"My horse is mighty tired," said Rivers, "And a good deal thirstier. Can you do anything about it?"

"Sure, stranger," said the bar-keep.

Sam bustled away into a back room, shouted some orders to one of his workers there, and returned half a minute later.

"Now you can give yourself some attention," he said. "What can we git you?"

"Food and plenty of it," said Rivers. "Ain't eaten in a while."

Sam made himself busy, thinking he had never seen anybody more in need of food. For Skinny Rivers was tall and raw-boned, and gave the false impression that he was thin, though beneath his dusty clothes he had muscle enough for hard work. He might have been more impressive if he had carried a bit more breadth to his height, and his nose not been quite so lop-sided in the way it had healed after a break. But there was a light in his eyes that suggested quiet confidence.

Rivers rubbed the bump on the side of his nose as he looked about him. There were several cow-punchers at the tables, but their drinks had barely been touched and they were all staring morosely, seemingly at nothing at all.

Sam came round the bar with a plate heaped with steaming vegetables and a large slice of beef.

"Thanks," said Rivers, "I'll be needin' another like it."

Sam's eyebrows lifted sharply towards his bald brow.

176

"You saying you'll be needin' *two* like that?"

"Sure. Then an apple pie, mebbe."

"If you say so stranger. The customer's always right in these parts."

Rivers, his mouth already full, indicated the silent, glum-faced occupants of the room.

"What's the trouble with them?" he demanded. "Somebody poisoned the beer?"

"Nope."

"Then what's making 'em look that way? They couldn't look worse if somebody 'd shot the President."

Rivers transferred a forkful of potato to his mouth. It was a large mouth, Sam noticed, and good-humored, for the moment.

"It's the fight. Folks round here were backing Iron-Fist Carmichael," Sam explained. "Gone and done the most tomfool thing. Tumbled from his nag and broke his wrist."

"I don't see why the town should go into mournin' on that account," said Rivers.

Mebbe not, but you're a stranger here. Carmichael was in the Western Territories Championship Fight, an' that broken wrist put him right out," said Sam miserably.

"I still, don't see any cause for the tears."

"It's like this," said the bar-keep. "There's no one in Holbrook who kin fight like Carmichael. He was our only hope of beatin' Gorilla O'Bannion, all the way from Santa Fe. The deal was, we here at Holbrook put up a man – any man – to beat the champ from Santa Fe. O'Bannion's manager's bin takin' our money all week an' we've bin keen to give it; we thought we had a good thing with our money ridin' on Iron-Fist Carmichael. Now we get to lose it without so much as a dog's chance."

Rivers nodded, understanding beginning to dawn on him.

"But surely Carmichael isn't the only one who can fight in this town?" he asked, surprised.

"'He's the only guy who kin use his fists sufficient to take O'Bannion. Now if the weapons'd been guns-"

"But they ain't," Rivers cut in, scratching the side of his broken nose, as a little smile appeared on his face. "But tell you what, buddy, if there's a bit of a prize, *I'll* fight Gorilla O'Bannion."

Sam's laugh had its origin somewhere in the depths of his large stomach. It rumbled up gathering sound as it came and then exploded in a thunderous roar.

Skinny Rivers, smiling slightly, ate several mouthfuls of meat and vegetables until Sam regained some measure of control.

"Say, now that was funny," Sam chuckled. "That shows you ain't never seen Gorilla O'Bannion."

"I've never even heard of him," Rivers admitted.

"Then I'll tell you one or two mighty interestin' things about him," Sam volunteered. "'He's twice your weight, I reckon, with the biggest arms an' chest I've ever seen, an' they're solid, stranger, as solid a rock."

"Uh-huh. And you reckon he can fight?" said Rivers.

"Fight? Say, now, the Gorilla's unbeaten in twenty-one fights," said Sam, "though we was pretty sure our man

178

Carmichael could take him."

"You don't say. Mighty interesting," the stranger in town said quietly. "And when is the fight billed to take place?"

"*Was* billed, you mean. Tonight, but as Iron-Fist Carmichael ain't able to use his right mitt there won't be no fight," said the bar-keep.

"An' that's why the boys look like committin' suicide in a bunch?"

"Yep," said Sam, "an' they've good reason to look that ways. They've just about bet all they have on Carmichael, an' they lose every dime they've wagered if the fight don't come off."

"But the fight *is* comin' off," Rivers insisted.

Sam regarded him in great perplexity, unable to make up his mind whether the lanky stranger meant him to take his remark seriously. Certainly Rivers looked serious enough, although he seemed still to be giving all his attention to his food.

"What's the prize money?" Rivers demanded of the still puzzled Sam.

"A thousand bucks for the winner – nix for the loser."

"Thousand dollars, eh?" Rivers drawled, pausing in the eating of his meal for the first time. "Well, as I'll be as near broke as makes no difference when I've paid for my eats, I'll have to win, I reckon."

Sam scratched his beard incredulously, his eyes bulging.

"Then you are serious, after all?"

"Sure I am," said Rivers. "I'll give it a shot."

Sam turned to the gloomy-faced punchers.

179

"He's goin' to do it," he stuttered, indicating Rivers with a downward pointing thumb.

"Goin' to do what?" a puncher asked carelessly.

"Fight Gorilla O'Bannion!" said Sam.

The punchers came to life as though stabbed deeply and simultaneously with long needles.

"Suffering cat-fish! Are you serious, mister?" said one.

"Sure," said Rivers, eating heartily again.

"Waal, I'll tell my Aunt Fanny!" said another. "What's yer name feller?"

"Rivers," he said, "Skinny Rivers."

This evoked a ripple of laughter from the saloon crowd. They detached themselves from their chairs and gathered about Rivers' chair, looking him over in pitying wonder.

"You'll take a mighty long coffin," said a check-shirted puncher.

"Assumin'," added a companion, "we can piece him back together after the Gorilla's finished with him."

There were some grim smiles, but no laughter.

"Take no notice," said Sam, "It's jus' their way o' not gettin' up their hopes too high. They got a fighter, but with respect, Mr Skinny Rivers, you ain't no Iron-Fist Carmichael!"

Rivers looked up from his food, annoyed, but said nothing.

"Somebody had better go along an' tell Percy Wanger," a bearded range-man said solemnly. Then he turned to Rivers to explain: "Percy's Holbrook's undertaker, buddy. I reck'n you'll be needin' his services purty soon. Shall I get him ter give yer a quick measurin' up, young feller?"

180

Rivers laughed easily.

"What makes you all so sure I'll get beaten up?" he enquired.

"We've seen the Gorilla fight before," the range-man answered. "That guy is mighty tough and big and quick. He mashed up poor ole Knuckler Soanes two years back, an' he ain't bin good fer nothin' since. As fer Rory Sugden last year, took two days fer him to wake up after the Gorilla put 'im out fer the count. Even now, his mind's, well, kinder confused."

"So you think the fight left a lastin' impression on Sugden's mind?" said Rivers.

"An everlastin' impression," was the range-man's solemn answer.

"Waal, I'm still goin' to fight," the stranger in town asserted quietly.

"Mister, you've guts, I'll say that," the check-shirted puncher acknowledged admiringly. "An' we sure hope you win. Only take my tip, if you've a wife an' kids anywhere, back out now. You're like ter get mess'd up good."

"I ain't got any dependants of any kind, and I'm not backing out," said Rivers determinedly. "An' if I were you, I'd quit runnin' down your own man. Seems to me I'm your only hope of gettin' a return on all that money you've laid out."

The punchers brightened up, not because they had any hope whatever that Rivers would beat the Gorilla, but they were heartened, at least, by the prospect of the fight, and grateful for the entertainment they would have.

"Now – where does the bout take place, and when?" Rivers asked.

"There's a ring fixed up at the back of the main street," Sam told him. The fight starts at six."

Rivers settled back, resting after his meal, and from time to time punchers and cattlemen came in to look at him curiously, and would go away solemnly shaking their heads. Rivers paid them no heed. His appetite satisfied, he was feeling pleasantly content.

"Sam," he said, after a time, "where do I find the Triple Hoop Ranch? I rode in to pick a job up there."

Sam took him through the batwing doors and pointed straight down the main street, away to a distant, low hill on the horizon.

"It's out there, Skinny, 'bout a mile," he said.

"Then I'll walk," Rivers decided. "I've got to keep myself loosened up for the fight, I guess."

# CHAPTER TWO:
## THE BULLY

Sam waved as the tall man set off down the street. It was even hotter than in the morning, but Rivers barely noticed the fact. His thumbs tucked into his belt, he walked easily, his long legs covering the ground quickly.

He had almost reached the end of the street, where the track that lead to the Triple Hoop Ranch began, when a boy of about twelve passed him, running lightly along the sidewalk. At the same moment, a burly figure came into view in a side-alley leading onto the main street. The boy and the man reached the corner at the same moment, the boy running full tilt into the man.

As the boy's head butted the man in the stomach, there was a surprised cry from the kid, and an angry grunt from the man.

The boy fell back, then regained his balance.

"I'm real sorry, Mr. Hogan, Sir," he stammered.

"You will be afore I've done wi' yer!" the man snarled, stepping forward and striking the boy heavily on the side of the head.

The boy lurched away, but Hogan's anger was not appeased, for he was about to follow up with a second blow when his arm was caught and held firmly in mid-air.

"I wouldn't do that if I were you, buddy," said Rivers.

Skinny Rivers' voice was very quiet, but there was no mistaking the determination in his manner.

"Why, you, son of a bitch!" said Hogan, jerking his arm

free. "I'll teach you to interfere!" he shouted.

Rivers had already noticed that Hogan was unusually well built. His chin was thickly bearded, and his hair bristled all over his head like the quills on a hedgehog. His neck was thick and short, and his body was built on similar lines. It was full-shouldered, and the arms were stout and long.

As he clenched his fists and advanced, eyes blazing, on Rivers, he looked frightful in his anger and formidableness.

"Uh-oh," thought Rivers, "the last thing I need now is a fight before I even get in the ring with Gorilla O'Bannion."

And so he determined to do everything in his power to avoid this man. But before he could try to appease him, Hogan lashed out furiously. Had the blow connected, Rivers would have been out for a very long time. The blow, however, whistled by his head as he swayed neatly out of its way.

"Hold your horses, mister, I've no wish to fight you," he said to the surprised Hogan.

"I'll bet you 'ain't, but ya goin' to, all the same," leered the man.

Rivers was dismayed. This was an encounter he would gladly have walked away from, if he were only given a chance by Hogan. The latter, however, had already flung off his coat, to reveal arms that bulged and were knotted with muscle. Rivers, therefore, had no alternative but to remove his own jacket, and he had only just done so when he was attacked again.

Rivers' jaw set, and he clenched his teeth. Hogan evidently was willing to take any mean advantage that might come his way, a fact which filled Skinny Rivers with cold anger.

This time, Hogan made no sudden dash. He came forward, obviously intending to time his blows. When his fist flashed out, it came with the speed of lightning, but Rivers ducked and stepped back.

He was only vaguely conscious of the rapidly thickening ring of spectators which, as if by magic, had gathered about Hogan and himself. His whole attention was fixed on this unwanted opponent.

Hogan's second failure seemed to have filled him with a towering rage. In the next few moments, Rivers found himself sparring with what might have been a tornado. The blows came so quickly and in such numbers that it was impossible to avoid them all, and he gasped when a blow caught him on the shoulder. His arm went numb for a few seconds, and it was then that he made up his mind to use all the science he knew in dealing with this Hogan.

Evidently, encouraged by his success, Hogan arrogantly imagined that the fight was as good as his. He advanced upon the slowly retreating Rivers, his arms smashing forward like flails. He was jolted back suddenly as River's fist caught him a heavy blow on the chest.

Astonished, he had barely recovered before he received three more punches, each one causing him to grunt with pain. It was his turn to fall back but only for a few steps. Recovering himself, he parried River's further punches, and the next moment the two men were circling each other warily, each looking for a likely opening.

The crowd, which had been roaring until now, were tensely silent, but Rivers was hardly aware of their presence. All his attention was now concentrated on Hogan, whose eyes flashed evilly. Rivers had the feeling that he was in unusually grave danger. There was something in Hogan's manner which warned him that there would be no mercy if he gained the upper hand. Rivers realised that he was looking straight into the face of a man capable of murder; and he knew only too well that many men had met their death in a bare-knuckle fight like this.

Both men were already perspiring freely, the sweat pouring down their faces and filming their bodies, and Rivers had already decided upon the strategy he must pursue. In the next five minutes the crowd saw him stepping, dodging and ducking, swaying out of Hogan's reach again and again, and making no effort to strike his opponent. They could see now, he had some considerable skill in the art boxing, but that wouldn't help him if the heavier man landed a big blow on his jaw.

The eyes of the crowd were almost popping out of their heads, for none there had ever seen such neat footwork. Hogan was quick, particularly in delivering his blows, but not once did he connect with Rivers face or body.

Sam Sturridge was dancing up and down, his fat cheeks bulging with excitement.

"Hit 'im, Skinny!" he kept shouting. "Hit the varmint!"

The crowd, in those moments when it broke the silence, shouted the same refrain:

"Hit 'im, Skinny! Hit 'im!"

Rivers, however, paid no heed. He was watching his adversary intently, not only to note the blows, but to see how he was drawing upon his reserves of wind and energy.

Hogan, however, though panting heavily, showed no signs of distress, and Rivers gritted his teeth still more firmly. The ground beneath their ever-moving feet was churned and trampled, and they were surrounded by a fine dust which hung languidly in the still air.

It was a piece of that gritty dust which settled in Rivers' eye. It stung his eye sharply, causing it to water. He blinked furiously, and in that moment Hogan sent his fist crashing into the lighter man's jaw. Lights flashed before River's eyes, but he had the presence of mind to go down instantly, falling like a log.

# CHAPTER THREE:
## THE SIDEWINDER!

The groan of dismay from the onlookers was stifled almost at once, for Rivers, with a quick shake of his head jumped to his feet again.

He knew, though, that he had to change his strategy, for his initial plan had been foiled by that speck of dust finding its way into his eye. Hogan's blow had robbed him of his advantages in speed and stamina that had allowed him to stand off his opponent somewhat. Now he would have to slug it out, trade blow for blow and hope to knock the bigger man down.

Casting aside his defensive policy, and much to the astonishment of the crowd, he went suddenly over to the attack. His maneuver caught Hogan unawares, and Rivers first blow landed squarely over his opponent's heart. It was followed by two more to the chest, and Hogan staggered back gasping. Recovering, be carried the fight back to Rivers and for thirty seconds they stood toe to toe hammering each other mercilessly.

A right from Rivers caught Hogan sharply on the right eye. Hogan went back quickly, shaking his head, but fortune as well as skill had favored Rivers. The eye had been too severely hit, and it began to swell and close immediately. Encouraged by this success, but still cautious, Rivers took full advantage. Feinting with his left, as though attempting a blow at Hogan's jaw, he brought his right forward with all his strength, and it smashed into Hogan, just above the solar plexus. Hogan staggered, trying to gulp in the urgently needed air which had been jolted out of him.

He was given no time to recover, however, for Rivers leapt forward and his fists beat a rapid tattoo on Hogan's body. Hogan swayed, and in that moment Rivers flashed a vicious uppercut to his jaw. Hogan's eyes went blank, he sagged suddenly, and then tumbled into the dust. Warily, Skinny Rivers stood over him, and waited.

Breathlessly, the crowd waited too. But Hogan made no effort to rise. Rivers bent down to look: and saw that his opponent's eyes were tightly closed.

At the same time a cheer went up from the crowd.

"Rivers has won it! Skinny Rivers won!" shouted the barkeep.

Sam Sturridge's cry was taken up by the crowd, which surged forward. Eager hands thumped Skinny Rivers on the shoulders.

But Rivers was looking dismayed. Now that he had time to think, he realised that the fight had cost him more than a few bruises and most of his energy.

"I reckon I won't be fighting the Gorilla tonight, Sam," he said sadly, "And I sure could have done with that thousand dollars."

"Fight the Gorilla tonight?" Sam echoed blankly, "Did you say you won't be able to?"

"Not likely, after dealing with Hogan," he said. "How could I?"

"But he *is* the Gorilla," Sam shouted. "Who else'd you think this hulk could be? Gorilla O'Bannion's his ring name, but rightly he's called Herbert Hogan."

A broad, relieved smile broke out on Rivers' face.

"It's the Gorilla who won't be able to fight," Sam told him exuberantly. "Besides, you beat him fair and square, whichever way you look on it, that means the boys have won their wagers and you've won the thousand bucks."

"Well knock me down with a feather!" said Rivers, almost too exhausted to stand.

"Hah!" said Sam, "Take more'n a feather to knock you down, young feller. Where'd you say you hail'd from?"

"I didn't," said Rivers, receiving a packet of money from a be-suited man – Hogan's manager – and heading for the saloon.

"I know the answer to that question," said a small, compact man in a cavalry soldier's uniform. "Seen him fight before."

"Oh yeah?" said Sam, focusing on the stranger. "Where?"

"U.S. Army Inter-Regimental boxing tournament," said the soldier, "down in Fort Defiance. That's Skinny 'Sidewinder' Rivers, won the cup two years runnin'. Got his discharge papers not three weeks ago. Said he was goin' professional. Funny he turned up here. Hell of a nice feller, but don't tangle with him. He may not look like much, but take it from me, the man's a *killer.*"

THE END

190

*Dear Reader,*
*If you have enjoyed these stories, please leave a review*
*on Amazon. Your feedback is greatly appreciated!*
*Best wishes,*
*Ed Garron*

## ALSO BY **ED GARRON:**

### WESTERNS 2:
# WILD AS THE WIND!

*Six Novellas of the Old Frontier including the*
*story of outlaw turned lawman Matty*
*McCray in 'The Plains of Arizona'*

### WESTERNS 3:
# BROTHER OF THE WOLF!

*An outlaw is pursued into the snow-covered*
*mountains by the forces of law and order...*

### WESTERNS 4:
# YARNS OF THE OPEN RANGE

*Cow-punchers share their true – & tall – stories...*

www.edgarron.com

**WILDCARD WESTERNS**
*In association with the* DERNFORD PRESS

Made in the USA
Monee, IL
22 December 2024

75083243R00114